KING ARTHUR
Tales of the Round Table

KING ARTHUR
Tales of the Round Table

EDITED BY ANDREW LANG

ILLUSTRATED BY H. J. FORD

SCHOCKEN BOOKS · NEW YORK

First published in 1902

First SCHOCKEN edition 1967
Third Printing, 1976
Library of Congress Catalog Card No. 67-26996

Manufactured in the United States of America

CONTENTS

	PAGE
The Drawing of the Sword	3
The Questing Beast	9
The Sword Excalibur	14
The Story of Sir Balin	16
How the Round Table began	25
The Passing of Merlin	31
How Morgan Le Fay tried to kill King Arthur	33
What Beaumains asked of the King	38
The Quest of the Holy Graal	64
The Fight for the Queen	102
The Fair Maid of Astolat	113
Lancelot and Guenevere	132
The End of it All	160

ILLUSTRATIONS

FULL-PAGE PLATES

How Arthur drew the Sword . . . . *to face p.*	4
Arthur and the Questing Beast . . . . „	10
Arthur meets the Lady of the Lake . . . „	14
The Death of Balin and Balan . . . . „	20
Merlin and Vivien . . . . . . „	31
Morgan Le Fay casts away the Scabbard . . „	34
Gareth and Linet . . . . „	42
Linet and the Black Knight . . . . „	46
The Lady of Lyonesse sees Sir Gareth . . „	54
Sir Galahad opens the Tomb . . . . „	72
Lancelot at the Chapel . . . . . . „	78
Sir Percivale slays the Serpent . . . . „	80
Lancelot and the Dwarf . . . . . „	96
Guenevere and Sir Bors . . . . . „	106
Arthur and Guenevere kiss before all the People . „	108
Elaine ties her Sleeve round Sir Lancelot's Helmet „	116
The Black Barget . . . . . . „	128
Lancelot brings Guenevere to Arthur . . . „	132
The Archers threaten Lancelot . . . . „	138
Lancelot bears off Guenevere . . . . „	154
Sir Mordred . . . . „	164
Excalibur returns to the Mere . . . . „	168

IN TEXT

	PAGE
The Damsel warns Sir Balin	19
How Sir Bors was saved from killing his Brother	89
Sir Mador accuses Guenevere	104
Guenevere sends her Page to Lancelot for Help	136
Lancelot comes out of Guenevere's Room	148

KING ARTHUR
Tales of the Round Table

THE DRAWING OF THE SWORD

Long, long ago, after Uther Pendragon died, there was no King in Britain, and every Knight hoped to seize the crown for himself. The country was like to fare ill when laws were broken on every side, and the corn which was to give the poor bread was trodden underfoot, and there was none to bring the evildoer to justice. Then, when things were at their worst, came forth Merlin the magician, and fast he rode to the place where the Archbishop of Canterbury had his dwelling. And they took counsel together, and agreed that all the lords and gentlemen of Britain should ride to London and meet on Christmas Day, now at hand, in the Great Church. So this was done. And on Christmas morning, as they left the church, they saw in the churchyard a large stone, and on it a bar of steel, and in the steel a naked sword was held, and about it was written in letters of gold, 'Whoso pulleth out this sword is by right of birth King of England.' They marvelled at these words, and called for the Archbishop, and brought him into the place where the stone stood. Then those Knights who fain would be King could not hold themselves back, and they tugged at the sword with all their might; but it never stirred. The Archbishop watched them in silence, but when they were faint from pulling he spoke: 'The man is not here who shall lift out that sword, nor do I know where to find him. But this is my counsel — that two Knights be chosen, good and true men, to keep guard over the sword.'

Thus it was done. But the lords and gentlemen-at-

arms cried out that every man had a right to try to win
the sword, and they decided that on New Year's Day a
tournament should be held, and any Knight who would,
might enter the lists.

So on New Year's Day, the Knights, as their custom
was, went to hear service in the Great Church, and
after it was over they met in the field to make ready for
the tourney.   Among them was a brave Knight called
Sir Ector, who brought with him Sir Kay, his son, and
Arthur, Kay's foster-brother.   Now Kay had unbuckled
his sword the evening before, and in his haste to be at
the tourney had forgotten to put it on again, and he
begged Arthur to ride back and fetch it for him.   But
when Arthur reached the house the door was locked, for
the women had gone out to see the tourney, and though
Arthur tried his best to get in he could not.   Then he
rode away in great anger, and said to himself, 'Kay shall
not be without a sword this day.   I will take that sword
in the churchyard, and give it to him'; and he galloped
fast till he reached the gate of the churchyard.   Here he
jumped down and tied his horse tightly to a tree, then,
running up to the stone, he seized the handle of the
sword, and drew it easily out; afterwards he mounted
his horse again, and delivered the sword to Sir Kay.   The
moment Sir Kay saw the sword he knew it was not his
own, but the sword of the stone, and he sought out his
father Sir Ector, and said to him, 'Sir, this is the sword
of the stone, therefore I am the rightful King.'   Sir
Ector made no answer, but signed to Kay and Arthur to
follow him, and they all three went back to the church.
Leaving their horses outside, they entered the choir, and
here Sir Ector took a holy book and bade Sir Kay swear
how he came by that sword.   'My brother Arthur gave
it to me,' replied Sir Kay.   'How did you come by it?'
asked Sir Ector, turning to Arthur.   'Sir,' said Arthur,
'when I rode home for my brother's sword I found no
one to deliver it to me, and as I resolved he should not

IVRE REX BRITANNIÆ

HOW ARTHVR DREW THE SWORD

be swordless I thought of the sword in this stone, and I pulled it out.' 'Were any Knights present when you did this?' asked Sir Ector. 'No, none,' said Arthur. 'Then it is you,' said Sir Ector, 'who are the rightful King of this land.' 'But why am I the King?' inquired Arthur. 'Because,' answered Sir Ector, 'this is an enchanted sword, and no man could draw it but he who was born a King. Therefore put the sword back into the stone, and let me see you take it out.' 'That is soon done,' said Arthur, replacing the sword, and Sir Ector himself tried to draw it, but he could not. 'Now it is your turn,' he said to Sir Kay, but Sir Kay fared no better than his father, though he tugged with all his might and main. 'Now you, Arthur,' and Arthur pulled it out as easily as if it had been lying in its sheath, and as he did so Sir Ector and Sir Kay sank on their knees before him. 'Why do you, my father and brother, kneel to me?' asked Arthur in surprise. 'Nay, nay, my lord,' answered Sir Ector, 'I was never your father, though till to-day I did not know who your father really was. You are the son of Uther Pendragon, and you were brought to me when you were born by Merlin himself, who promised that when the time came I should know from whom you sprang. And now it has been revealed to me.' But when Arthur heard that Sir Ector was not his father, he wept bitterly. 'If I am King,' he said at last, 'ask what you will, and I shall not fail you. For to you, and to my lady and mother, I owe more than to anyone in the world, for she loved me and treated me as her son.' 'Sir,' replied Sir Ector, 'I only ask that you will make your foster-brother, Sir Kay, Seneschal[1] of all your lands.' 'That I will readily,' answered Arthur, 'and while he and I live no other shall fill that office.'

Sir Ector then bade them seek out the Archbishop with him, and they told him all that had happened concerning the sword, which Arthur had left standing in the

---

[1] 'Seneschal' means steward.

stone. And on the Twelfth Day the Knights and Barons
came again, but none could draw it out but Arthur.
When they saw this, many of the Barons became angry
and cried out that they would never own a boy for King
whose blood was no better than their own. So it was
agreed to wait till Candlemas, when more Knights might
be there, and meanwhile the same two men who
had been chosen before watched the sword night and
day; but at Candlemas it was the same thing, and at
Easter. And when Pentecost came, the common people
who were present, and saw Arthur pull out the sword,
cried with one voice that he was their King, and they
would kill any man who said differently. Then rich and
poor fell on their knees before him, and Arthur took the
sword and offered it upon the altar where the Archbishop
stood, and the best man that was there made him Knight.
After that the crown was put on his head, and he swore
to his lords and commons that he would be a true King,
and would do them justice all the days of his life.

THE QUESTING BEAST

But Arthur had many battles to fight and many Kings to conquer before he was acknowledged lord of them all, and often he would have failed had he not listened to the wisdom of Merlin, and been helped by his sword Excalibur, which in obedience to Merlin's orders he never drew till things were going ill with him. Later it shall be told how the King got the sword Excalibur, which shone so bright in his enemies' eyes that they fell back, dazzled by the brightness. Many Knights came to his standard, and among them Sir Ban, King of Gaul beyond the sea, who was ever his faithful friend. And it was in one of these wars, when King Arthur and King Ban and King Bors went to the rescue of the King of Cameliard, that Arthur saw Guenevere, the King's daughter, whom he afterwards wedded. By and by King Ban and King Bors returned to their own country across the sea, and the King went to Carlion, a town on the river Usk, where a strange dream came to him.

He thought that the land was over-run with gryphons and serpents which burnt and slew his people, and he made war on the monsters, and was sorely wounded, though at last he killed them all. When he awoke the remembrance of his dream was heavy upon him, and to shake it off he summoned his Knights to hunt with him, and they rode fast till they reached a forest. Soon they spied a hart before them, which the King claimed as his game, and he spurred his horse and rode after him. But the hart ran fast and the King could not get near it, and the chase lasted so long that the King himself grew heavy and his horse fell dead under him. Then he sat under a tree and rested, till he heard the baying of hounds, and fancied he counted as many as thirty of them. He raised his head to look, and, coming towards him, saw a beast so strange that its like was not to be found throughout his kingdom. It went straight to the well and drank, making as it did so the noise of many hounds baying, and when it had drunk its fill the beast went its way.

While the King was wondering what sort of a beast this could be, a Knight rode by, who, seeing a man lying under a tree, stopped and said to him: 'Knight full of thought and sleepy, tell me if a strange beast has passed this way?'

'Yes, truly,' answered Arthur, 'and by now it must be two miles distant. What do you want with it?'

'Oh sir, I have followed that beast from far,' replied he, 'and have ridden my horse to death. If only I could find another I would still go after it.' As he spoke a squire came up leading a fresh horse for the King, and when the Knight saw it he prayed that it might be given to him, 'for,' said he, 'I have followed this quest this twelvemonth, and either I shall slay him or he will slay me.'

'Sir Knight,' answered the King, 'you have done your part; leave now your quest, and let me follow the beast for the same time that you have done.' 'Ah, fool!' replied the Knight, whose name was Pellinore, 'it would be all in vain, for none may slay that beast but I or my next of kin'; and without more words he sprang into the saddle. 'You may take my horse by force,' said the King, 'but I should like to prove first which of us two is the better horseman.'

'Well,' answered the Knight, 'when you want me, come to this spring. Here you will always find me,' and, spurring his horse, he galloped away. The King watched

ARTHVR·AND·THE·QUESTING·BEAST

him till he was out of sight, then turned to his squire and bade him bring another horse as quickly as he could. While he was waiting for it the wizard Merlin came along in the likeness of a boy, and asked the King why he was so thoughtful.

'I may well be thoughtful,' replied the King, 'for I have seen the most wonderful sight in all the world.'

'That I know well,' said Merlin, 'for I know all your thoughts. But it is folly to let your mind dwell on it, for thinking will mend nothing. I know, too, that Uther Pendragon was your father, and your mother was the Lady Igraine.'

'How can a boy like you know that?' cried Arthur, growing angry; but Merlin only answered, 'I know it better than any man living,' and passed, returning soon after in the likeness of an old man of fourscore, and sitting down by the well to rest.

'What makes you so sad?' asked he.

'I may well be sad,' replied Arthur, 'there is plenty to make me so. And besides, there was a boy here who told me things that he had no business to know, and among them the names of my father and mother.'

'He told you the truth,' said the old man, 'and if you would have listened he could have told you still more: how that your sister shall have a child who shall destroy you and all your Knights.'

'Who are you?' asked Arthur, wondering.

'I am Merlin, and it was I who came to you in the likeness of a boy. I know all things; how that you shall die a noble death, being slain in battle, while my end will be shameful, for I shall be put alive into the earth.'

There was no time to say more, for the man brought up the King's horse and he mounted, and rode fast till he came to Carlion.

THE SWORD EXCALIBUR

KING ARTHUR had fought a hard battle with the tallest Knight in all the land, and though he struck hard and well, he would have been slain had not Merlin enchanted the Knight and cast him into a deep sleep, and brought the King to a hermit who had studied the art of healing, and cured all his wounds in three days. Then Arthur and Merlin waited no longer, but gave the hermit thanks and departed.

As they rode together Arthur said, 'I have no sword,' but Merlin bade him be patient and he would soon give him one. In a little while they came to a large lake, and in the midst of the lake Arthur beheld an arm rising out of the water, holding up a sword. 'Look!' said Merlin, 'that is the sword I spoke of.' And the King looked again, and a maiden stood upon the water. 'That is the Lady of the Lake,' said Merlin, 'and she is coming to you, and if you ask her courteously she will give you the sword.' So when the maiden drew near Arthur saluted her and said, 'Maiden, I pray you tell me whose sword is that which an arm is holding out of the water? I wish it were mine, for I have lost my sword.'

'That sword is mine, King Arthur,' answered she, 'and I will give it to you, if you in return will give me a gift when I ask you.'

'By my faith,' said the King, 'I will give you whatever gift you ask.' 'Well,' said the maiden, 'get into the

14

ARTHVR MEETS THE LADY OF THE LAKE AND GETS THE SWORD EXCALIBVR

barge yonder, and row yourself to the sword, and take it and the scabbard with you.' For this was the sword Excalibur. 'As for *my* gift, I will ask it in my own time.' Then King Arthur and Merlin dismounted from their horses and tied them up safely, and went into the barge, and when they came to the place where the arm was holding the sword Arthur took it by the handle, and the arm disappeared. And they brought the sword back to land. As they rode the King looked lovingly on his sword, which Merlin saw, and, smiling, said, 'Which do you like best, the sword or the scabbard?' 'I like the sword,' answered Arthur. 'You are not wise to say that,' replied Merlin, 'for the scabbard is worth ten of the sword, and as long as it is buckled on you you will lose no blood, however sorely you may be wounded.' So they rode into the town of Carlion, and Arthur's Knights gave them a glad welcome, and said it was a joy to serve under a King who risked his life as much as any common man.

THE STORY OF SIR BALIN

In those days many Kings reigned in the Islands of the Sea, and they constantly waged war upon each other, and on their liege lord, and news came to Arthur that Ryons, King of North Wales, had collected a large host and had ravaged his lands and slain some of his people. When he heard this, Arthur rose in anger, and commanded that all lords, Knights, and gentlemen of arms should meet him at Camelot, where he would call a council, and hold a tourney.

From every part the Knights flocked to Camelot, and the town was full to overflowing of armed men and their horses. And when they were all assembled, there rode in a damsel, who said she had come with a message from the great Lady Lile of Avelion, and begged that they would bring her before King Arthur. When she was led into his presence she let her mantle of fur slip off her shoulders, and they saw that by her side a richly wrought sword was buckled. The King was silent with wonder at the strange sight, but at last he said, 'Damsel, why do you wear this sword? for swords are not the ornaments of women.' 'Oh, my lord,' answered she, 'I would I could find some Knight to rid me of this sword, which weighs me down and causes me much sorrow. But the man who will deliver me of it must be one who is mighty of his hands, and pure in his deeds, without villainy, or treason. If I find a Knight such as this, he will draw this sword out of its sheath,

16

and he only. For I have been at the Court of King
Ryons, and he and his Knights tried with all their strength
to draw the sword and they could not.'

'Let me see if I can draw it,' said Arthur, 'not
because I think myself the best Knight, for well I know
how far I am outdone by others, but to set them an
example that they may follow me.' With that the King
took the sword by the sheath and by the girdle, and
pulled at it with all his force, but the sword stuck fast.
'Sir,' said the damsel, 'you need not pull half so hard,
for he that shall pull it out shall do it with little strength.'
'It is not for me,' answered Arthur, 'and now, my Barons,
let each man try his fortune.' So most of the Knights
of the Round Table there present pulled, one after
another, at the sword, but none could stir it from its
sheath. 'Alas! alas!' cried the damsel in great grief, 'I
thought to find in this Court Knights that were blameless
and true of heart, and now I know not where to look for
them.' 'By my faith,' said Arthur, 'there are no better
Knights in the world than these of mine, but I am sore
displeased that they cannot help me in this matter.'

Now at that time there was a poor Knight at Arthur's
Court who had been kept prisoner for a year and a
half because he had slain the King's cousin. He was
of high birth and his name was Balin, and after he had
suffered eighteen months the punishment of his misdeed
the Barons prayed the King to set him free, which
Arthur did willingly. When Balin, standing apart,
beheld the Knights one by one try the sword, and
fail to draw it, his heart beat fast, yet he shrank from
taking his turn, for he was meanly dressed, and could not
compare with the other Barons. But after the damsel
had bid farewell to Arthur and his Court, and was setting
out on her journey homewards, he called to her and said,
'Damsel, I pray you to suffer me to try your sword, as
well as these lords, for though I am so poorly clothed,
my heart is as high as theirs.' The damsel stopped and

looked at him, and answered, ' Sir, it is not needful to put
you to such trouble, for where so many have failed it is
hardly likely that you will succeed.'   ' Ah ! fair damsel,'
said Balin, ' it is not fine clothes that make good deeds.'
' You speak truly,' replied the damsel, ' therefore do what
you can.'   Then Balin took the sword by the girdle and
sheath, and pulled it out easily, and when he looked at
the sword he was greatly pleased with it.   The King and
the Knights were dumb with surprise that it was Balin
who had triumphed over them, and many of them envied
him and felt anger towards him.   ' In truth,' said the
damsel, ' this is the best Knight that I ever found, but,
Sir, I pray you give me the sword again.'

' No,' answered Balin, ' I will keep it till it is taken
from me by force.'   ' It is for your sake, not mine, that I
ask for it,' said the damsel, ' for with that sword you shall
slay the man you love best, and it shall bring about your
own ruin.'   ' I will take what befalls me,' replied Balin,
' but the sword I will not give up, by the faith of my
body.'   So the damsel departed in great sorrow.   The
next day Sir Balin left the Court, and, armed with his
sword, set forth in search of adventures, which he found
in many places where he had not thought to meet with
them.   In all the fights that he fought, Sir Balin was the
victor, and Arthur, and Merlin his friend, knew that
there was no Knight living of greater deeds, or more
worthy of worship.   And he was known to all as Sir Balin
le Savage, the Knight of the two swords.

One day he was riding forth when at the turning of a
road he saw a cross, and on it was written in letters of
gold, ' Let no Knight ride towards this castle.'   Sir Balin
was still reading the writing when there came towards
him an old man with white hair, who said, ' Sir Balin le
Savage, this is not the way for you, so turn again and
choose some other path.'   And so he vanished, and a
horn blew loudly, as a horn is blown at the death of a
beast.   ' That blast,' said Balin, ' is for me, but I am still

alive,' and he rode to the castle, where a great company
of Knights and ladies met him and welcomed him, and

The Damsel Warns Sir Balin.

made him a feast. Then the lady of the castle said to
him, 'Knight with the two swords, you must now fight a

Knight that guards an island, for it is our law that no man may leave us without he first fight a tourney.'

'.That is a bad custom,' said Balin, 'but if I must I am ready; for though my horse is weary my heart is strong.'

'Sir,' said a Knight to him, 'your shield does not look whole to me ; I will lend you another'; so Balin listened to him and took the shield that was offered, and left his own with his own coat of arms behind him. He rode down to the shore, and led his horse into a boat, which took them across. When he reached the other side, a damsel came to him crying, 'O Knight Balin, why have you left your own shield behind you? Alas! you have put yourself in great danger, for by your shield you should have been known. I grieve over your doom, for there is no man living that can rival you for courage and bold deeds.'

'I repent,' answered Balin, 'ever having come into this country, but for very shame I must go on. Whatever befalls me, either for life or death, I am ready to take it.' Then he examined his armour, and saw that it was whole, and mounted his horse.

As he went along the path he beheld a Knight come out of a castle in front, clothed in red, riding a horse with red trappings. When this red Knight looked on the two swords, he thought for a moment it was Balin, but the shield did not bear Balin's device. So they rode at each other with their spears, and smote each other's shields so hard that both horses and men fell to the ground with the shock, and the Knights lay unconscious on the ground for some minutes. But soon they rose up again and began the fight afresh, and they fought till the place was red with their blood, and they had each seven great wounds. 'What Knight are you ? ' asked Balin le Savage, pausing for breath, ' for never before have I found any Knight to match me.' 'My name,' said he, 'is Balan, brother to the good Knight Balin.'

The Death of Balin and Balan

'Alas!' cried Balin, 'that I should ever live to see this day,' and he fell back fainting to the ground. At this sight Balan crept on his feet and hands, and pulled off Balin's helmet, so that he might see his face. The fresh air revived Balin, and he awoke and said: 'O Balan, my brother, you have slain me, and I you, and the whole world shall speak ill of us both.'

'Alas,' sighed Balan, 'if I had only known you! I saw your two swords, but from your shield I thought you had been another Knight.'

'Woe is me!' said Balin, 'all this was wrought by an unhappy Knight in the castle, who caused me to change my shield for his. If I lived, I would destroy that castle that he should not deceive other men.'

'You would have done well,' answered Balan, 'for they have kept me prisoner ever since I slew a Knight that guarded this island, and they would have kept you captive too.' Then came the lady of the castle and her companions, and listened as they made their moan. And Balan prayed that she would grant them the grace to lie together, there where they died, and their wish was given them, and she and those that were with her wept for pity.

So they died; and the lady made a tomb for them, and put Balan's name alone on it, for Balin's name she knew not. But Merlin knew, and next morning he came and wrote it in letters of gold, and he ungirded Balin's sword, and unscrewed the pommel, and put another pommel on it, and bade a Knight that stood by handle it, but the Knight could not. At that Merlin laughed. 'Why do you laugh?' asked the Knight. 'Because,' said Merlin, 'no man shall handle this sword but the best Knight in the world, and that is either Sir Lancelot or his son Sir Galahad. With this sword Sir Lancelot shall slay the man he loves best, and Sir Gawaine is his name.' And this was later done, in a fight across the seas.

All this Merlin wrote on the pommel of the sword.

Next he made a bridge of steel to the island, six inches broad, and no man could pass over it that was guilty of any evil deeds. The scabbard of the sword he left on this side of the island, so that Galahad should find it. The sword itself he put in a magic stone, which floated down the stream to Camelot, that is now called Winchester. And the same day Galahad came to the river, having in his hand the scabbard, and he saw the sword and pulled it out of the stone, as is told in another place.

HOW THE ROUND TABLE BEGAN

It was told in the story of the Questing Beast that King Arthur married the daughter of Leodegrance, King of Cameliard, but there was not space there to say how it came about. And as the tales of the Round Table are full of this lady, Queen Guenevere, it is well that anybody who reads this book should learn how she became Queen.

After King Arthur had fought and conquered many enemies, he said one day to Merlin, whose counsel he took all the days of his life, 'My Barons will let me have no rest, but bid me take a wife, and I have answered them that I shall take none, except you advise me.'

'It is well,' replied Merlin, 'that you should take a wife, but is there any woman that you love better than another?' 'Yes,' said Arthur, 'I love Guenevere, daughter of Leodegrance, King of Cameliard, in whose house is the Round Table that my father gave him. This maiden is the fairest that I have ever seen, or ever shall see.' 'Sir,' answered Merlin, 'what you say as to her beauty is true, but, if your heart was not set on her, I could find you another as fair, and of more goodness, than she. But if a man's heart is once set it is idle to try to turn him.' Then Merlin asked the King to give him a company of Knights and esquires, that he might go to the Court of King Leodegrance and tell him that King Arthur desired to wed his daughter, which Arthur did gladly. Therefore Merlin rode forth and made all the haste he could till he came to the Castle of Cameliard, and told King Leodegrance who had sent him and why.

'That is the best news I have ever had,' replied Leodegrance, 'for little did I think that so great and noble a King should seek to marry my daughter. As for lands to endow her with, I would give whatever he chose; but he has lands enough of his own, so I will give him instead something that will please him much more, the Round Table which Uther Pendragon gave me, where a hundred and fifty Knights can sit at one time. I myself can call to my side a hundred good Knights, but I lack fifty, for the wars have slain many, and some are absent.' And without more words King Leodegrance gave his consent that his daughter should wed King Arthur. And Merlin returned with his Knights and esquires, journeying partly by water and partly by land, till they drew near to London.

When King Arthur heard of the coming of Merlin and of the Knights with the Round Table he was filled with joy, and said to those that stood about him, 'This news that Merlin has brought me is welcome indeed, for I have long loved this fair lady, and the Round Table is dearer to me than great riches.' Then he ordered that Sir Lancelot should ride to fetch the Queen, and that preparations for the marriage and her coronation should be made, which was done. 'Now, Merlin,' said the King, 'go and look about my kingdom and bring fifty of the bravest and most famous Knights that can be found throughout the land.' But no more than eight and twenty Knights could Merlin find. With these Arthur had to be content, and the Bishop of Canterbury was fetched, and he blessed the seats that were placed by the Round Table, and the Knights sat in them. 'Fair Sirs,' said Merlin, when the Bishop had ended his blessing, 'arise all of you, and pay your homage to the King.' So the Knights arose to do his bidding, and in every seat was the name of the Knight who had sat on it, written in letters of gold, but two seats were empty. After that young Gawaine came to the King, and prayed him to make him a Knight on the day that he should wed Guenevere. 'That I will gladly,' replied the King, 'for you are my sister's son.'

As the King was speaking, a poor man entered the Court, bringing with him a youth about eighteen years old, riding on a lean mare, though it was not the custom for gentlemen to ride on mares. 'Where is King Arthur?' asked the man. 'Yonder,' answered the Knights. 'Have you business with him?' 'Yes,' said the man, and he went and bowed low before the King: 'I have heard, O King Arthur, flower of Knights and Kings, that at the time of your marriage you would give any man the gift he should ask for.'

'That is truth,' answered the King, 'as long as I do no wrong to other men or to my kingdom.'

'I thank you for your gracious words,' said the poor man; 'the boon I would ask is that you would make my son a Knight.' 'It is a great boon to ask,' answered the King. 'What is your name?'

'Sir, my name is Aries the cowherd.'

'Is it you or your son that has thought of this honour?'

'It is my son who desires it, and not I,' replied the man. 'I have thirteen sons who tend cattle, and work in the fields if I bid them; but this boy will do nothing but shoot and cast darts, or go to watch battles and look on Knights, and all day long he beseeches me to bring him to you, that he may be knighted also.'

'What is your name?' said Arthur, turning to the young man.

'Sir, my name is Tor.'

'Where is your sword that I may knight you?' said the King.

'It is here, my lord.'

'Take it out of its sheath,' said the King, 'and

require me to make you a Knight.' Then Tor jumped off his mare and pulled out his sword, and knelt before the King, praying that he might be made a Knight and a Knight of the Round Table.

'As for a Knight, that I will make you,' said Arthur, smiting him in the neck with the sword, 'and if you are worthy of it you shall be Knight of the Round Table.' And the next day he made Gawaine Knight also.

MERLIN and VIVIEN

THE PASSING OF MERLIN

Sir Tor proved before long by his gallant deeds that he was worthy to sit in one of the two empty seats of the Round Table. Many of the other Knights went out also in search of adventures, and one of them, Sir Pellinore, brought a damsel of the lake to Arthur's Court, and when Merlin saw her he fell in love with her, so that he desired to be always in her company. The damsel laughed in secret at Merlin, but made use of him to tell her all she would know, and the wizard had no strength to say her nay, though he knew what would come of it. For he told King Arthur that before long he should be put into the earth alive, for all his cunning. He likewise told the King many things that should befall him, and warned him always to keep the scabbard as well as the sword Excalibur, and foretold that both sword and scabbard should be stolen from him by a woman whom he most trusted. 'You will miss my counsel sorely,' added Merlin, 'and would give all your lands to have me back again.' 'But since you know what will happen,' said the King, 'you may surely guard against it.' 'No,' answered Merlin, 'that will not be.' So he departed from the King, and the maiden followed him whom some call Nimue and others Vivien, and wherever she went Merlin went also.

They journeyed together to many places, both at home and across the seas, and the damsel was wearied of him, and sought by every means to be rid of him, but he would not be shaken off. At last these two wandered back to

Cornwall, and one day Merlin showed Vivien a rock under which he said great marvels were hidden. Then Vivien put forth all her powers, and told Merlin how she longed to see the wonders beneath the stone, and, in spite of all his wisdom, Merlin listened to her and crept under the rock to bring forth the strange things that lay there. And when he was under the stone she used the magic he had taught her, and the rock rolled over him, and buried him alive, as he had told King Arthur. But the damsel departed with joy, and thought no more of him : now that she knew all the magic he could teach her.

HOW MORGAN LE FAY TRIED TO KILL KING ARTHUR

KING ARTHUR had a sister called Morgan le Fay, who was skilled in magic of all sorts, and hated her brother because he had slain in battle a Knight whom she loved. But to gain her own ends, and to revenge herself upon the King, she kept a smiling face, and let none guess the passion in her heart.

One day Morgan le Fay went to Queen Guenevere, and asked her leave to go into the country. The Queen wished her to wait till Arthur returned, but Morgan le Fay said she had had bad news and could not wait. Then the Queen let her depart without delay.

Early next morning at break of day Morgan le Fay mounted her horse and rode all day and all night, and at noon next day reached the Abbey of nuns where King Arthur had gone to rest, for he had fought a hard battle, and for three nights had slept but little. 'Do not wake him,' said Morgan le Fay, who had come there knowing she would find him, 'I will rouse him myself when I think he has had enough sleep,' for she thought to steal his sword Excalibur from him. The nuns dared not disobey her, so Morgan le Fay went straight into the room where King Arthur was lying fast asleep in his bed, and in his right hand was grasped his sword Excalibur. When she beheld that sight, her heart fell, for she dared not touch the sword, knowing well that if Arthur waked and saw her she was a dead woman. So she took the scabbard, and went away on horseback.

When the King awoke and missed his scabbard, he was angry, and asked who had been there; and the nuns told him that it was his sister, Morgan le Fay, who had gone away with a scabbard under her mantle. 'Alas!' said Arthur, 'you have watched me badly!'

'Sir,' said they, 'we dared not disobey your sister.'

'Saddle the best horse that can be found,' commanded the King, 'and bid Sir Ontzlake take another and come with me.' And they buckled on their armour and rode after Morgan le Fay.

They had not gone far before they met a cowherd, and they stopped to ask if he had seen any lady riding that way. 'Yes,' said the cowherd, 'a lady passed by here, with forty horses behind her, and went into the forest yonder.' Then they galloped hard till Arthur caught sight of Morgan le Fay, who looked back, and, seeing that it was Arthur who gave chase, pushed on faster than before. And when she saw she could not escape him, she rode into a lake that lay in the plain on the edge of the forest, and, crying out, 'Whatever may befall me, my brother shall not have the scabbard,' she threw the scabbard far into the water, and it sank, for it was heavy with gold and jewels. After that she fled into a valley full of great stones, and turned herself and her men and her horses into blocks of marble. Scarcely had she done this when the King rode up, but seeing her nowhere thought some evil must have befallen her in vengeance for her misdeeds. He then sought high and low for the scabbard, but could not find it, so he returned unto the Abbey. When Arthur was gone, Morgan le Fay turned herself and her horses and her men back into their former shapes, and said, 'Now, Sirs, we may go where we will.' And she departed into the country of Gore, and made her towns and castles stronger than before, for she feared King Arthur greatly. Meanwhile King Arthur had rested himself at the Abbey, and afterwards he rode to Camelot, and was welcomed by

MORGAN LE FAY CASTS AWAY THE SCABBARD

his Queen and all his Knights. And when he told his adventures and how Morgan le Fay sought his death they longed to burn her for her treason.

The next morning there arrived a damsel at the Court with a message from Morgan le Fay, saying that she had sent the King her brother a rich mantle for a gift, covered with precious stones, and begged him to receive it and to forgive her in whatever she might have offended him. The King answered little, but the mantle pleased him, and he was about to throw it over his shoulders when the lady of the lake stepped forward, and begged that she might speak to him in private. 'What is it?' asked the King. 'Say on here, and fear nothing.' 'Sir,' said the lady, 'do not put on this mantle, or suffer your Knights to put it on, till the bringer of it has worn it in your presence.' 'Your words are wise,' answered the King, 'I will do as you counsel me. Damsel, I desire you to put on this mantle that you have brought me, so that I may see it.' 'Sir,' said she, 'it does not become me to wear a King's garment.' 'By my head,' cried Arthur, 'you shall wear it before I put it on my back, or on the back of any of my Knights,' and he signed to them to put it on her, and she fell down dead, burnt to ashes by the enchanted mantle. Then the King was filled with anger, more than he was before, that his sister should have dealt so wickedly by him.

WHAT BEAUMAINS ASKED OF THE KING

As Pentecost drew near King Arthur commanded that all the Knights of the Round Table should keep the feast at a city called Kin-Kenadon, hard by the sands of Wales, where there was a great castle. Now it was the King's custom that he would eat no food on the day of Pentecost, which we call Whitsunday, until he had heard or seen some great marvel. So on that morning Sir Gawaine was looking from the window a little before noon when he espied three men on horseback, and with them a dwarf on foot, who held their horses when they alighted. Then Sir Gawaine went to the King and said, 'Sir, go to your food, for strange adventures are at hand.' And Arthur called the other Kings that were in the castle, and all the Knights of the Round Table that were a hundred and fifty, and they sat down to dine. When they were seated there entered the hall two men well and richly dressed, and upon their shoulders leaned the handsomest young man that ever was seen of any of them, higher than the other two by a cubit. He was wide in the chest and large handed, but his great height seemed to be a burden and a shame to him, therefore it was he leaned on the shoulders of his friends. As soon as Arthur beheld him he made a sign, and without more words all three went up to the high daïs, where the King sat. Then the tall young man stood up straight, and said: 'King Arthur, God bless you and all your fair fellowship, and in especial the fellowship of the Table Round. I have come hither to pray you to give me three gifts, which you can grant

me honourably, for they will do no hurt to you or to anyone.' 'Ask,' answered Arthur, 'and you shall have your
asking.'

'Sir, this is my petition for this feast, for the other
two I will ask after. Give me meat and drink for this
one twelvemonth.' 'Well,' said the King, 'you shall
have meat and drink enough, for that I give to every
man, whether friend or foe. But tell me your name!'

'I cannot tell you that,' answered he. 'That is
strange,' replied the King, 'but you are the goodliest young
man I ever saw,' and, turning to Sir Kay, the steward,
charged him to give the young man to eat and drink of
the best, and to treat him in all ways as if he were a
lord's son. 'There is little need to do that,' answered
Sir Kay, 'for if he had come of gentlemen and not of
peasants he would have asked of you a horse and
armour. But as the birth of a man is so are his requests.
And seeing he has no name I will give him one, and it
shall be Beaumains, or Fair-hands, and he shall sit in the
kitchen and eat broth, and at the end of a year he shall
be as fat as any pig that feeds on acorns.' So the young
man was left in charge of Sir Kay, that scorned and
mocked him.

Sir Lancelot and Sir Gawaine were wroth when they
heard what Sir Kay said, and bade him leave off his
mocking, for they believed the youth would turn out
to be a man of great deeds; but Sir Kay paid no heed
to them, and took him down to the great hall, and
set him among the boys and lads, where he ate sadly.
After he had finished eating both Sir Lancelot and Sir
Gawaine bade him come to their room, and would have
had him eat and drink there, but he refused, saying he
was bound to obey Sir Kay, into whose charge the King
had given him. So he was put into the kitchen by Sir
Kay, and slept nightly with the kitchen boys. This he
bore for a whole year, and was always mild and gentle,
and gave hard words to no one. Only, whenever the

Knights played at tourney he would steal out and watch
them.   And Sir Lancelot gave him gold to spend, and
clothes to wear, and so did Gawaine.   Also, if there were
any games held whereat he might be, none could throw
a bar nor cast a stone as far as he by two good yards.

Thus the year passed by till the feast of Whitsuntide
came again, and this time the King held it at Carlion.
But King Arthur would eat no meat at Whitsuntide till
some adventures were told him, and glad was he when a
squire came and said to him, 'Sir, you may go to your
food, for here is a damsel with some strange tales.'   At
this the damsel was led into the hall, and bowed low
before the King, and begged he would give her help.
'For whom?' asked the King, 'and what is the adventure?   'Sir,' answered she, 'my sister is a noble lady
of great fame, who is besieged by a tyrant, and may not
get out of her castle.   And it is because your Knights are
said to be the noblest in all the world that I came to
you for aid.'   'What is your sister's name, and where does
she dwell?   And who is the man that besieges her, and
where does he come from?'   'Sir King,' answered she,
'as for my sister's name, I cannot tell it you now, but she
is a lady of great beauty and goodness, and of many lands.
As for the tyrant who besieges her, he is called the Red
Knight of the Red Lawns.'   'I know nothing of him,'
said the King.   'But I know him,' cried Sir Gawaine,
'and he is one of the most dangerous Knights in the
world.   Men say he has the strength of seven, and once
when we had crossed swords I hardly escaped from him
with my life.'   'Fair damsel,' then said the King, 'there
are many Knights here who would go gladly to the rescue
of your lady, but none of them shall do so with my consent unless you will tell us her name, and the place of
her castle.'   'Then I must speak further,' said the damsel.
But before she had made answer to the King up came
Beaumains, and spoke to Arthur, saying, 'Sir King, I
thank you that for this whole year I have lived in your

kitchen, and had meat and drink, and now I will ask you
for the two gifts that you promised me on this day.'
'Ask them,' answered the King. 'Sir, this shall be my
two gifts. First grant me the adventure of this damsel,
for it is mine by right.' 'You shall have it,' said the
King. 'Then, Sir, you shall bid Sir Lancelot du Lake
to make me Knight, for I will receive knighthood at the
hands of no other.' 'All this shall be done,' said the
King. 'Fie on you,' cried the damsel, 'will you give me
none but a kitchen boy to rescue my lady?' and she went
away in a rage, and mounted her horse.

No sooner had she left the hall than a page came to
Beaumains and told him that a horse and fair armour
had been brought for him, also there had arrived a dwarf
carrying all things that a Knight needed. And when he
was armed there were few men that were handsomer
than he, and the Court wondered greatly whence these
splendid trappings had come. Then Beaumains came
into the hall, and took farewell of the King, and Sir
Gawaine and Sir Lancelot, and prayed Sir Lancelot that
he would follow after him. So he departed, and rode
after the damsel. Many looked upon him and marvelled
at the strength of his horse, and its golden trappings, and
envied Beaumains his shining coat of mail; but they
noted that he had neither shield nor spear. 'I will ride
after him,' laughed Sir Kay, 'and see if my kitchen boy
will own me for his better.' 'Leave him and stay at
home,' said Sir Gawaine and Sir Lancelot, but Sir Kay
would not listen and sprang upon his horse. Just as
Beaumains came up with the damsel, Sir Kay reached
Beaumains, and said, 'Beaumains, do you not know
me?'

Beaumains turned and looked at him, and answered,
'Yes, I know you for an ill-mannered Knight, therefore
beware of me.' At this Sir Kay put his spear in rest
and charged him, and Beaumains drew his sword and
charged Sir Kay, and dashed aside the spear, and thrust

him through the side, till Sir Kay fell down as if he
had been dead,. and Beaumains took his shield and
spear for himself. Then he sprang on his own horse,
bidding first his dwarf take Sir Kay's horse, and rode
away. All this was seen by Sir Lancelot, who had
followed him, and also by the damsel. In a little while
Beaumains stopped, and asked Sir Lancelot if he would
tilt with him, and they came together with such a
shock that both the horses and their riders fell to the
earth and were bruised sorely. Sir Lancelot was the
first to rise, and he helped Beaumains from his horse,
and Beaumains threw his shield from him, and offered
to fight on foot. And they rushed together like wild
boars, turning and thrusting and parrying for the space
of an hour, and Sir Lancelot marvelled at the young
man's strength, and thought he was more like a giant than
a Knight, and dreading lest he himself should be put to
shame, he said : ' Beaumains, do not fight so hard, we
have no quarrel that forbids us to leave off.' 'That is
true,' answered Beaumains, laying down his arms, ' but
it does me good, my lord, to feel your might.' 'Well,
said Sir Lancelot, 'I promise you I had much ado to
save myself from you unshamed, therefore have no fear of
any other Knight.' 'Do you think I could really stand
against a proved Knight ? ' asked Beaumains. 'Yes,'
said Lancelot, ' if you fight as you have fought to-day I
will be your warrant against anyone.' 'Then I pray you,'
cried Beaumains, 'give me the order of knighthood.'
'You must first tell me your name,' replied Lancelot,
' and who are your kindred.' 'You will not betray me if
I do ? ' asked Beaumains. 'No, that I will never do, till
it is openly known,' said Lancelot. 'Then, Sir, my name
is Gareth, and Sir Gawaine is my brother.' 'Ah, Sir,'
cried Lancelot, 'I am gladder of you than ever I was, for
I was sure you came of good blood, and that you did not
come to the Court for meat and drink only.' And he
bade him kneel, and gave him the order of knighthood.

Faugh Sir! You smell of ye Kitchen

Gareth & Linet

After that Sir Gareth wished to go his own ways, and departed. When he was gone, Sir Lancelot went back to Sir Kay and ordered some men that were by to bear him home on a shield, and in time his wounds were healed; but he was scorned of all men, and especially of Sir Gawaine and Sir Lancelot, who told him it was no good deed to treat any young man so, and no one could tell what his birth might be, or what had brought him to the Court.

Then Beaumains rode after the damsel, who stopped when she saw him coming. 'What are you doing here?' said she. 'Your clothes smell of the grease and tallow of the kitchen! Do you think to change my heart towards you because of yonder Knight whom you slew? No, truly! I know well who you are, you turner of spits! Go back to King Arthur's kitchen, which is your proper place.' 'Damsel,' replied Beaumains, 'you may say to me what you will, but I shall not quit you whatever you may do, for I have vowed to King Arthur to relieve the lady in the castle, and I shall set her free or die fighting for her.' 'Fie on you, Scullion,' answered she. 'You will meet with one who will make you such a welcome that you would give all the broth you ever cooked never to have seen his face.' 'I shall do my best to fight him,' said Beaumains, and held his peace.

Soon they entered the wood, and there came a man flying towards them, galloping with all his might. 'Oh, help! help! lord,' cried he, 'for my master lies in a thicket, bound by six thieves, and I greatly fear they will slay him.' 'Show me the way,' said Sir Beaumains, and they rode together till they reached the place where the Knight lay bound. Then Sir Beaumains charged the six thieves, and struck one dead, and another, and another still, and the other three fled, not liking the battle. Sir Beaumains pursued them till they turned at bay, and fought hard for their lives; but in the end Sir Beaumains slew them, and returned to the Knight and unbound him. The Knight thanked Beaumains heartily for his deliverance, and prayed him to come to his castle, where he would reward him. 'Sir,' said Beaumains, 'I was this day made Knight by noble Sir Lancelot, and that is reward enough for anything I may do. Besides, I must follow this damsel.' But when he came near her she reviled him as before, and bade him ride far from her. 'Do you think I set store by what you have done? You will soon see a sight that will make you tell a very different tale.' At this the Knight whom Beaumains had rescued rode up to the damsel, and begged that she would rest in his castle that night, as the sun was now setting. The damsel agreed, and the Knight ordered a great supper, and gave Sir Beaumains a seat above the seat of the damsel, who rose up in anger. 'Fie! fie! Sir Knight,' cried she, 'you are uncourteous to set a mere kitchen page before me; he is not fit to be in the company of high-born people.' Her words struck shame into the Knight, and he took Beaumains and set him at a side table, and seated himself before him.

In the early morning Sir Beaumains and the damsel bade farewell to the Knight, and rode through the forest till they came to a great river, where stood two Knights on the further side, guarding the passage. 'Well, what do you say now?' asked the damsel. 'Will you fight them or turn back?' 'I would not turn if there were six more of them,' answered Sir Beaumains, and he rushed into the water and so did one of the Knights. They came together in the middle of the stream, and their spears broke in two with the force of the charge, and they drew their swords, hitting hard at each other. At length Sir Beaumains dealt the other Knight such a blow that he fell from his horse, and was drowned in the river. Then Beaumains put his horse at the bank, where the second Knight was waiting for him, and they fought long together, till Sir Beaumains clave his helmet in two.

LINET AND THE BLACK KNIGHT

So he left him dead, and rode after the damsel. 'Alas!' she cried, 'that even a kitchen page should have power to destroy two such Knights! You think you have done mighty things, but you are wrong! As to the first Knight, his horse stumbled, and he was drowned before you ever touched him. And the other you took from behind, and struck him when he was defenceless.' 'Damsel!' answered Beaumains, 'you may say what you will, I care not what it is, so I may deliver this lady.' 'Fie, foul kitchen knave, you shall see Knights that will make you lower your crest.' 'I pray you be more civil in your language,' answered Beaumains, 'for it matters not to me what Knights they be, I will do battle with them.' 'I am trying to turn you back for your own good,' answered she, 'for if you follow me you are certainly a dead man, as well I know all you have won before has been by luck.' 'Say what you will, damsel,' said he, 'but where you go I will follow you,' and they rode together till eventide, and all the way she chid him and gave him no rest.

At length they reached an open space where there was a black lawn, and on the lawn a black hawthorn, whereon hung a black banner on one side, and a black shield and spear, big and long, on the other. Close by stood a black horse covered with silk, fastened to a black stone. A Knight, covered with black armour, sat on the horse, and when she saw him the damsel bade him ride away, as his horse was not saddled. But the Knight drew near and said to her, 'Damsel, have you brought this Knight from King Arthur's Court to be your champion?' 'No, truly,' answered she, 'this is but a kitchen boy, fed by King Arthur for charity.' 'Then why is he clad in armour?' asked the Knight; 'it is a shame that he should even bear you company.' 'I cannot be rid of him,' said she, 'he rides with me against my will. I would that you were able to deliver me from him! Either slay him or frighten him off, for by ill fortune he has this day slain the two Knights of the passage.' 'I wonder much,' said the Black Knight, 'that any man who is well born should consent to fight with him.' 'They do not know him,' replied the damsel, 'and they think he must be a famous Knight because he rides with me.' 'That may be,' said the Black Knight, 'but he is well made, and looks likely to be a strong man; still I promise you I will just throw him to the ground, and take away his horse and armour, for it would be a shame to me to do more.' When Sir Beaumains heard him talk thus he looked up and said, 'Sir Knight, you are lightly disposing of my horse and armour, but I would have you know that I will pass this lawn, against your will or not, and you will only get my horse and armour if you win them in fair fight. Therefore let me see what you can do.' 'Say you so?' answered the Knight, 'now give up the lady at once, for it ill becomes a kitchen page to ride with a lady of high degree.' 'It is a lie,' said Beaumains, 'I am a gentleman born, and my birth is better than yours, as I will prove upon your body.'

With that they drew back their horses so as to charge each other hotly, and for the space of an hour and a half they fought fiercely and well, but in the end a blow from Beaumains threw the Knight from his horse, and he swooned and died. Then Beaumains jumped down, and seeing that the Knight's horse and armour were better than his own, he took them for himself, and rode after the damsel. While they were thus riding together, and the damsel was chiding him as ever she did, they saw a Knight coming towards them dressed all in green. 'Is that my brother the Black Knight who is with you?' asked he of the damsel. 'No, indeed,' she replied, 'this unhappy kitchen knave has slain your brother, to my great sorrow.' 'Alas!' sighed the Green Knight, 'that my brother should die so meanly at the hand of a kitchen knave. Traitor!' he added, turning to Beaumains, 'thou shalt die for slaying my brother, for he was a noble Knight, and his name was Sir Percard.' 'I defy you,' said Beaumains, 'for I slew him as a good Knight should.'

Then the Green Knight seized a horn which hung from a horn tree, and blew three notes upon it, and two damsels came and armed him, and fastened on him a green shield and a green spear. So the fight began and raged long, first on horseback and then on foot, till both were sore wounded. At last the damsel came and stood beside them, and said, 'My lord the Green Knight, why for very shame do you stand so long fighting a kitchen knave? You ought never to have been made a Knight at all!' These scornful words stung the heart of the Green Knight, and he dealt a mighty stroke which cleft asunder the shield of Beaumains. And when Beaumains saw this, he struck a blow upon the Knight's helmet which brought him to his knees, and Beaumains leapt on him, and dragged him to the ground. Then the Green Knight cried for mercy, and offered to yield himself prisoner unto Beaumains. 'It is all in vain,' answered Beaumains, 'unless the damsel prays me for your life,' and therewith he unlaced his helmet as though he would slay him. 'Fie upon thee, false kitchen page!' said the damsel, 'I will never pray to save his life, for I am sure he is in no danger.' 'Suffer me not to die,' entreated the Knight, 'when a word may save me!' 'Fair Knight,' he went on, turning to Beaumains, 'save my life, and I will forgive you the death of my brother, and will do you service for ever, and will bring thirty of my Knights to serve you likewise.' 'It is a shame,' cried the damsel, 'that such a kitchen knave should have you and thirty Knights besides.' 'Sir Knight,' said Beaumains, 'I care nothing for all this, but if I am to spare your life the damsel must ask for it,' and he stepped forward as if to slay him. 'Let be, foul knave,' then said the damsel, 'do not slay him. If you do, you will repent it.' 'Damsel,' answered Beaumains, 'it is a pleasure to me to obey you, and at your wish I will save his life. Sir Knight with the green arms, I release you at the request of this damsel, and I will fulfil all she charges me.'

Then the Green Knight kneeled down, and did him homage with his sword. 'I am sorry,' said the damsel, 'for the wounds you have received, and for your brother's death, for I had great need of you both, and have much dread of passing the forest.' 'Fear nothing,' answered the Green Knight, 'for this evening you shall lodge in my house, and to-morrow I will show you the way through the forest.' And they went with the Green Knight. But the damsel did not mend her ways with Beaumains, and ever more reviled him, till the Green Knight rebuked her, saying Beaumains was the noblest Knight that held a spear, and that in the end she would find he had sprung from some great King. And the Green Knight summoned the thirty Knights who did him service, and bade them henceforth do service to Beaumains, and keep him from treachery, and when he had need of them they would be ready to obey his orders. So they bade each other farewell, and Beaumains and the damsel rode forth anew. In like manner did Sir Beaumains overcome the Red Knight, who was the third brother, and the Red Knight cried for mercy, and offered to bring sixty Knights to do him service, and Beaumains spared his life at the request of the damsel, and likewise it so happened to Sir Persant of Inde.

And this time the damsel prayed Beaumains to give up the fight, saying, 'Sir, I wonder who you are and of what kindred you have come. Boldly you speak, and boldly you have done; therefore I pray you to depart and save yourself while you may, for both you and your horse have suffered great fatigues, and I fear we delay too long, for the besieged castle is but seven miles from this place, and all the perils are past save this one only. I dread sorely lest you

should get some hurt; yet this Sir Persant of Inde is
nothing in might to the Knight who has laid siege to my
lady.' But Sir Beaumains would not listen to her words,
and vowed that by two hours after noon he would have
overthrown him, and that it would still be daylight when
they reached the castle. 'What sort of a man can you
be?' answered the damsel, looking at him in wonder,
'for never did a woman treat a Knight as ill and shamefully as I have done you, while you have always been
gentle and courteous to me, and no one bears himself
like that save he who is of noble blood.' 'Damsel,'
replied Beaumains, 'your hard words only drove me to
strike the harder, and though I ate in King Arthur's
kitchen, perhaps I might have had as much food as I
wanted elsewhere. But all I have done was to make
proof of my friends, and whether I am a gentleman or
not, fair damsel, I have done you gentleman's service,
and may perchance do you greater service before we part
from each other.' 'Alas, fair Beaumains, forgive me all
that I have said and done against you.' 'With all my
heart,' he answered, 'and since you are pleased now to
speak good words to me, know that I hear them gladly,
and there is no Knight living but I feel strong enough to
meet him.'

So Beaumains conquered Sir Persant of Inde, who
brought a hundred Knights to be sworn into his service,
and the next morning the damsel led him to the castle,
where the Red Knight of the Red Lawn held fast the
lady. 'Heaven defend you,' cried Sir Persant, when
they told him where they were going; 'that is the most
perilous Knight now living, for he has the strength
of seven men. He has done great wrong to that lady,
who is one of the fairest in all the world, and it seems to
me as if this damsel must be her sister. Is not her name
Linet?' 'Yes, Sir,' answered she, 'and my lady my
sister's name is dame Lyonesse.' 'The Red Knight has
drawn out the siege for two years,' said Sir Persant,

'though he might have forced an entrance many a time, but he hoped that Sir Lancelot du Lake or Sir Tristram or Sir Gawaine should come to do battle with him.' 'My Lord Sir Persant of Inde,' said the damsel, 'I bid you knight this gentleman before he fight with the Red Knight.' 'That I will gladly,' replied Sir Persant, 'if it please him to take the order of knighthood from so simple a man as I am.' 'Sir,' answered Beaumains, 'I thank you for your goodwill, but at the beginning of this quest I was made a Knight by Sir Lancelot. My name is Sir Gareth of Orkney and Sir Gawaine is my brother, though neither he nor King Arthur, whose sister is my mother, knows of it. I pray you to keep it close also.'

Now word was brought unto the besieged lady by the dwarf that her sister was coming to her with a Knight sent by King Arthur. And when the lady heard all that Beaumains had done, and how he had overthrown all who stood in his way, she bade her dwarf take baked venison, and fat capons, and two silver flagons of wine and a gold cup, and put them into the hands of a hermit that dwelt in a hermitage close by. The dwarf did so, and the lady then sent him to greet her sister and Sir Beaumains, and to beg them to eat and drink in the hermit's cell, and rest themselves, which they did. When they drew near the besieged castle Sir Beaumains saw full forty Knights, with spurs on their heels and swords in their hands, hanging from the tall trees that stood upon the lawn. 'Fair Sir,' said the damsel, 'these Knights came hither to rescue my sister, dame Lyonesse; and if you cannot overthrow the Knight of the Red Lawn, you will hang there too.'

'Truly,' answered Beaumains, 'it is a marvel that none of King Arthur's Knights has dealt with the Knight of the Red Lawn ere this'; and they rode up to the castle, which had round it high walls and deep ditches, till they came to a great sycamore tree, where hung a

The Lady of Lyonesse
sees Sir Gareth

horn. And whoso desired to do battle with the Red
Knight must blow that horn loudly.

'Sir, I pray you,' said Linet, as Beaumains bent forward to seize it, 'do not blow it till it is full noontide, for
during three hours before that the Red Knight's strength
so increases that it is as the strength of seven men; but
when noon is come, he has the might of one man only.'

'Ah! for shame, damsel, to say such words. I will
fight him as he is, or not at all,' and Beaumains blew
such a blast that it rang through the castle And the
Red Knight buckled on his armour, and came to where
Beaumains stood. So the battle began, and a fierce one
it was, and much ado had Beaumains to last out till noon,
when the Red Knight's strength began to wane; they
rested, and came on again, and in the end the Red
Knight yielded to Sir Beaumains, and the lords and
Barons in the castle did homage to the victor, and begged
that the Red Knight's life might be spared on condition
they all took service with Beaumains. This was granted
to them, and Linet bound up his wounds and put oint-
ment on them, and so she did likewise to Sir Beaumains.
But the Red Knight was sent to the Court of King Arthur,
and told him all that Sir Beaumains had done. And
King Arthur and his Knights marvelled.

Now Sir Beaumains had looked up at the windows of
Castle Perilous before the fight, and had seen the face of
the Lady Lyonesse, and had thought it the fairest in all
the world. After he had subdued the Red Knight, he
hasted into the castle, and the Lady Lyonesse welcomed
him, and he told her he had bought her love with the best
blood in his body. And she did not say him nay, but
put him off for a time. Then the King sent letters to her
to bid her, and likewise Sir Gareth, come to his Court,
and by the counsel of Sir Gareth she prayed the King
to let her call a tournament, and to proclaim that the
Knight who bore himself best should, if he was unwedded,
take her and all her lands. But if he had a wife already

he should be given a white ger-falcon, and for his wife a crown of gold, set about with precious stones.

So the Lady Lyonesse did as Sir Gareth had counselled her, and answered King Arthur that where Sir Gareth was she could not tell, but that if the King would call a tourney he might be sure that Sir Gareth would come to it. 'It is well thought of,' said Arthur, and the Lady Lyonesse departed unto Castle Perilous, and summoned all her Knights around her, and told them what she had done, and how they were to make ready to fight in the tournament. She began at once to set her castle in order, and to think what she should do with the great array of Knights that would ride hither from the furthest parts — from Scotland and Wales and Cornwall — and to lodge fitly the Kings, Dukes, Earls, and Barons that should come with Arthur. Queen Guenevere also she awaited, and the Queen of Orkney, Sir Gareth's mother. But Sir Gareth entreated the Lady Lyonesse and those Knights that were in the castle with him not to let his name be known, and this they agreed to.

'Sir Gareth,' said dame Lyonesse, 'I will lend you a ring, which I beseech you for the love you bear me to give me back when the tournament is done, for without it I have but little beauty. This ring is like no other ring, it will turn green red, and blue white, and the bearer shall lose no blood, however sore he may be wounded.'

'Truly, my own lady,' answered Sir Gareth, 'this ring will serve me well, and by its help I shall not fear that any man shall know me.' And Sir Gringamore, brother to the Lady Lyonesse, gave him a bay horse, and strong armour, and a sharp sword that had once belonged to his father. On the morning of the fifteenth of August, when the Feast of the Assumption was kept, the King commanded his heralds to blow loudly their trumpets, so that every Knight might know that he must enter the lists. It was a noble sight to see them flocking clad in shining armour, each man with his device upon his shield. And

the heralds marked who bare them best, and who were
overthrown. All marvelled as to who the Knight could be
whose armour sometimes seemed green, and sometimes
white, but no man knew it was Sir Gareth. And whoso-
ever Sir Gareth tilted with was straightway overthrown.
'Of a truth,' cried King Arthur, 'that Knight with the
many colours is a good Knight,' and he called Sir
Lancelot and bade him to challenge that Knight to
combat. But Sir Lancelot said that though the Knight
had come off victor in every fight, yet his limbs must be
weary, for he had fought as a man fights under the eyes
of his lady, 'and for this day,' said Sir Lancelot, 'he shall
have the honour. Though it lay in my power to put it
from him, I would not.'

Then they paused for a while to rest, and afterwards
the tournament began again more fiercely than before,
and Sir Lancelot was set upon by two Knights at once.
When Sir Gareth saw that, he rode in between them, but
no stroke would he deal Sir Lancelot, which Sir Lancelot
noted, and guessed that it was the good Knight, Sir Gareth.
Sir Gareth went hither and thither, smiting anyone that
came in his way, and by fortune he met with his brother Sir
Gawaine, and knocked off his helmet. Now it happened
that while he was fighting a Knight dealt Sir Gareth a
fierce blow on his helm, and he rode off the field to mend
it. Then his dwarf, who had been watching eagerly,
cried out to Sir Gareth to leave the ring with him, lest he
should lose it while he was drinking, which Sir Gareth
did; and when he had drunk and mended his helm he
forgot the ring, at which the dwarf was glad, for he knew
his name could no longer be hid. And when Sir Gareth
returned to the field, his armour shone yellow like gold,
and King Arthur marvelled what Knight he was, for he
saw by his hair that he was the same Knight who had
worn the many colours. 'Go,' he said to his heralds,
'ride near him and see what manner of Knight he is, for
none can tell me his name.' So a herald drew close to

him, and saw that on his helm was written in golden letters
'This helm belongs to Sir Gareth of Orkney'; and the
herald cried out and made proclamation, and the Kings
and Knights pressed to behold him. And when Sir
Gareth saw he was discovered, he struck more fiercely
than before, and smote down Sir Sagramore, and his
brother, Sir Gawaine. 'O brother,' said Sir Gawaine,
'I did not think you would have smitten me!' When
Sir Gareth heard him say that he rode out of the press,
and cried to his dwarf, 'Boy, you have played me foul,
for you have kept my ring. Give it to me now, that I may
hide myself,' and he galloped swiftly into the forest, and no
one knew where he had gone. 'What shall I do next?'
asked he of the dwarf. 'Sir,' answered the dwarf, 'send
the Lady Lyonesse back her ring.' 'Your counsel is good,'
said Gareth; 'take it to her, and commend me to her grace,
and say I will come when I may, and bid her to be faithful to me, as I am to her.' After that Sir Gareth rode
deeper into the forest.

Though Sir Gareth had left the tournament he found
that there were as many fights awaiting him as if he had
remained there. He overcame all his foes, and sent them
and their followers to do homage to King Arthur, but he
himself stayed behind. He was standing alone after they
had gone, when he beheld an armed Knight coming towards him. Sir Gareth sprang on his horse, and without
a word the two crashed together like thunder, and strove
hard for two hours, till the ground was wet with blood.
At that time the damsel Linet came riding by, and saw
what was doing, and knew who were the fighters. And
she cried, 'Sir Gawaine, Sir Gawaine, leave fighting with
your brother Sir Gareth.' Then he threw down his shield
and sword, and ran to Sir Gareth, and first took him in
his arms and next kneeled down and asked mercy of him.
'Why do you, who were but now so strong and mighty,
so suddenly yield to me?' asked Sir Gareth, who had not
perceived the damsel. 'O Gareth, I am your brother, and

have had much sorrow for your sake.' At this Sir Gareth
unlaced his helm and knelt before Sir Gawaine, and they
rose and embraced each other. 'Ah, my fair brother,'
said Sir Gawaine, 'I ought rightly to do you homage, even
if you were not my brother, for in this twelvemonth you
have sent King Arthur more Knights than any six of the
best men of the Round Table.' While he was speaking
there came the Lady Linet, and healed the wounds of
Sir Gareth and of Sir Gawaine. 'What are you going to
do now?' asked she. 'It is time that King Arthur had
tidings of you both, and your horses are not fit to bear
you.'

'Ride, I pray you,' said Sir Gawaine, 'to my uncle,
King Arthur, who is but two miles away, and tell him
what adventure has befallen me.' So she mounted her
mule, and when she had told her tale to King Arthur, he
bade them saddle him a palfrey and invited all the
Knights and ladies of his Court to ride with him. When
they reached the place they saw Sir Gareth and Sir
Gawaine sitting on the hill-side. The King jumped off
his horse, and would have greeted them, but he swooned
away for gladness, and they ran and comforted him, and
also their mother.

The two Knights stayed in King Arthur's Court for
eight days, and rested themselves and grew strong. Then
said the King to Linet, 'I wonder that your sister, dame
Lyonesse, does not come here to visit me, or more truly
to visit my nephew, Sir Gareth, who has worked so hard
to win her love.'

'My lord,' answered Linet, 'you must, by your grace,
hold her excused, for she does not know that Sir Gareth
is here.'

'Go and fetch her, then,' said Arthur.

'That I will do quickly,' replied Linet, and by the
next morning she had brought dame Lyonesse, and her
brother Sir Gringamore, and forty Knights, but among the
ladies dame Lyonesse was the fairest, save only Queen

Guenevere. They were all welcomed of King Arthur, who turned to his nephew Sir Gareth and asked him whether he would have that lady to his wife.

'My lord,' replied Sir Gareth, 'you know well that I love her above all the ladies in the world.'

'And what say you, fair lady?' asked the King.

'Most noble King,' said dame Lyonesse, 'I would sooner have Sir Gareth as my husband than any King or Prince that may be christened, and if I may not have him I promise you I will have none. For he is my first love, and shall be my last. And if you will suffer him to have his will and choice, I dare say he will have me.'

'That is truth,' said Sir Gareth.

'What, nephew,' cried the King, 'sits the wind in that door? Then you shall have all the help that is in my power,' and so said Gareth's mother. And it was fixed that the marriage should be at Michaelmas, at Kin-Kenadon by the sea-shore, and thus it was proclaimed in all places of the realm. Then Sir Gareth sent his summons to all the Knights and ladies that he had won in battle that they should be present, and he gave a rich ring to the Lady Lyonesse, and she gave him one likewise. And before she departed she had from King Arthur a shining golden bee, as a token. After that Sir Gareth set her on her way towards her castle, and returned unto the King. But he would ever be in Sir Lancelot's company, for there was no Knight that Sir Gareth loved so well as Sir Lancelot. The days drew fast to Michaelmas, and there came the Lady Lyonesse with her sister Linet and her brother Sir Gringamore to Kin-Kenadon by the sea, and there were they lodged by order of King Arthur. And upon Michaelmas Day the Bishop of Canterbury wedded Sir Gareth and the Lady Lyonesse with great ceremonies, and King Arthur commanded that Sir Gawaine should be joined to the damsel Linet, and Sir Agrawaine to the niece of dame Lyonesse, whose name was Laurel. Then the Knights whom Sir

Gareth had won in battle came with their followings and did homage to him, and the Green Knight besought him that he might act as chamberlain at the feast, and the Red Knight that he might be his steward. As soon as the feast was ended, they had all manner of minstrelsy and games and a great tournament that lasted three days, but at the prayer of dame Lyonesse the King would not suffer that any man who was wedded should fight at that feast.

THE QUEST OF THE HOLY GRAAL

THIS is a mysterious part of the adventures of King Arthur's Knights. We must remember that parts of these stories are very old; they were invented by the heathen Welsh, or by the ancient Britons, from whom the Welsh are descended, and by the old pagan Irish, who spoke Gaelic, a language not very unlike Welsh. Then these ancient stories were translated by French and other foreign writers, and Christian beliefs and chivalrous customs were added in the French romances, and, finally, the French was translated into English about the time of Edward IV. by Sir Thomas Malory, who altered as he pleased. The Story of the Holy Graal, in this book, is mostly taken from Malory, but partly from ' The High History of the Holy Graal,' translated by Dr. Sebastian Evans from an old French book.

What *was* the Holy Graal? In the stories it is the holy vessel used by our Lord, and brought to Britain by Joseph of Arimathea. But in the older heathen Irish stories there is a mysterious vessel of a magical sort, full of miraculous food, and probably the French writers of the romances confused this with the sacred vessel brought from the Holy Land. On account of the sins of men this relic was made invisible, but now and then it appeared, borne by angels or floating in a heavenly light. The Knights, against King Arthur's wish, made a vow to find it, and gave up their duties of redressing wrongs and keeping order, to pursue the beautiful vision. But most of them, for their sins, were unsuccessful, like Sir

Lancelot, and the Round Table was scattered and the kingdom was weakened by the neglect of ordinary duties in the search for what could never be gained by mortal men. This appears to be the moral of the story, if it has any moral. But the stories are confused almost like a dream, though it is a beautiful dream.

I

HOW THE KING WENT ON PILGRIMAGE, AND HIS SQUIRE WAS SLAIN IN A DREAM

Now the King was minded to go on a pilgrimage, and he agreed with the Queen that he would set forth to seek the holy chapel of St. Augustine, which is in the White Forest, and may only be found by adventure. Much he wished to undertake the quest alone, but this the Queen would not suffer, and to do her pleasure he consented that a youth, tall and strong of limb, should ride with him as his squire. Chaus was the youth's name, and he was son to Gwain li Aoutres. 'Lie within to-night,' commanded the King, 'and take heed that my horse be saddled at break of day, and my arms ready.' 'At your pleasure, Sir,' answered the youth, whose heart rejoiced because he was going alone with the King.

As night came on, all the Knights quitted the hall, but Chaus the squire stayed where he was, and would not take off his clothes or his shoes, lest sleep should fall on him and he might not be ready when the King called him. So he sat himself down by the great fire, but in spite of his will sleep fell heavily on him, and he dreamed a strange dream.

In his dream it seemed that the King had ridden away to the quest, and had left his squire behind him, which filled the young man with fear. And in his dream he set the saddle and bridle on his horse, and fastened his spurs, and girt on his sword, and galloped out of the castle after the King. He rode on a long space, till he entered a thick forest, and there before him lay traces of the King's horse, and he followed till the marks of the hoofs ceased suddenly at some open ground and he thought that the King had alighted there. On the right stood a chapel, and about it was a graveyard, and in the graveyard many coffins, and in his dream it seemed as if the King had entered the chapel, so the young man entered also. But no man did he behold save a Knight that lay dead upon a bier in the midst of the chapel, covered with a pall of rich silk, and four tapers in golden candlesticks were burning round him. The squire marvelled to see the body lying there so lonely, with no one near it, and likewise that the King was nowhere to be seen. Then he took out one of the tall tapers, and hid the candlestick under his cloak, and rode away until he should find the King.

On his journey through the forest he was stopped by a man black and ill-favoured, holding a large knife in his hand.

'Ho! you that stand there, have you seen King Arthur?' asked the squire.

'No, but I have met you, and I am glad thereof, for you have under your cloak one of the candlesticks of gold that was placed in honour of the Knight who lies dead in the chapel. Give it to me, and I will carry it back; and if you do not this of your own will, I will make you.'

'By my faith!' cried the squire, 'I will never yield it to you! Rather, will I carry it off and make a present of it to King Arthur.'

'You will pay for it dearly,' answered the man, 'if you yield it not up forthwith.'

To this the squire did not make answer, but dashed forward, thinking to pass him by; but the man thrust at him with his knife, and it entered his body up to the hilt. And when the squire dreamed this, he cried, 'Help! help! for I am a dead man!'

As soon as the King and the Queen heard that cry they awoke from their sleep, and the Chamberlain said, 'Sir, you must be moving, for it is day'; and the King rose and dressed himself, and put on his shoes. Then the cry came again: 'Fetch me a priest, for I die!' and the King ran at great speed into the hall, while the Queen and the Chamberlain followed him with torches and candles. 'What aileth you?' asked the King of his squire, and the squire told him of all that he had dreamed. 'Ha,' said the King, 'is it, then, a dream?' 'Yes, Sir,' answered the squire, 'but it is a right foul dream for me, for right foully it hath come true,' and he lifted his left arm, and said, 'Sir, look you here! Lo, here is the knife that was struck in my side up to the haft.' After that, he drew forth the candlestick, and showed it to the King. 'Sir, for this candlestick that I present to you was I wounded to the death!' The King took the candlestick in his hands and looked at it, and none so rich had he seen before, and he bade the Queen look also. 'Sir,' said the squire again, ' draw not forth the knife out of my body till I be shriven of the priest.' So the King commanded that a priest should be sent for, and when the squire had confessed his sins, the King drew the knife out of the body and the soul departed forthwith. Then the King grieved that the young man had come to his death in such strange wise, and ordered him a fair burial, and desired that the golden candlestick should be sent to the Church of St. Paul in London, which at that time was newly built.

After this King Arthur would have none to go with him on his quest, and many strange adventures he achieved before he reached the chapel of St. Augustine, which was in the midst of the White Forest. There he alighted from his horse, and sought to enter, but though there was neither door nor bar he might not pass the threshold. But from without he heard wondrous voices singing, and saw a light shining brighter than any that he had seen before, and visions such as he scarcely dared to look upon. And he resolved greatly to amend his sins, and to bring peace and order into his kingdom. So he set forth, strengthened and comforted, and after divers more adventures returned to his Court.

II

THE COMING OF THE HOLY GRAAL

It was on the eve of Pentecost that all the Knights of the Table Round met together at Camelot, and a great feast was made ready for them. And as they sat at supper they heard a loud noise, as of the crashing of thunder, and it seemed as if the roof would fall on them. Then, in the midst of the thunder, there entered a sunbeam, brighter by seven times than the brightest day, and its brightness was not of this world. The Knights held their peace, but every man looked at his neighbour, and his countenance shone fairer than ever it had done before. As they sat dumb, for their tongues felt as if they could speak nothing, there floated in the hall the Holy Graal, and over it a veil of white samite, so that none might see it nor who bare it. But sweet odours filled the place, and every Knight had set before him the food he loved best; and after that the Holy Vessel departed suddenly, they wist not where. When it had gone their tongues were loosened, and the King gave thanks for the wonders that they had been permitted to see. After that he had finished, Sir Gawaine stood up and vowed to depart the next morning in quest of the Holy Graal, and not to return until he had seen it. 'But if after a year and a day I may not speed in my quest,' said he, 'I shall come again, for I shall know that the sight of it is not for me.' And many of the Knights there sitting swore a like vow.

But King Arthur, when he heard this, was sore displeased. 'Alas!' cried he unto Sir Gawaine, 'you have undone me by your vow. For through you is broken up the fairest fellowship, and the truest of knighthood, that ever the world saw, and when they have once departed they shall meet no more at the Table Round, for many shall die in the quest. It grieves me sore, for I have loved them as well as my own life.' So he spoke, and paused, and tears came into his eyes. 'Ah, Gawaine, Gawaine! you have set me in great sorrow.'

'Comfort yourself,' said Sir Lancelot, 'for we shall win for ourselves great honour, and much more than if we had died in any other wise, since die we must.' But the King would not be comforted, and the Queen and all the Court were troubled also for the love which they had to these Knights. Then the Queen came to Sir Galahad, who was sitting among those Knights, though younger he was than any of them, and asked him whence he came, and of what country, and if he was son to Sir Lancelot. And King Arthur did him great honour, and he rested him in his own bed. And next morning the King and Queen went into the Minster, and the Knights followed them, dressed all in armour, save only their shields and their helmets. When the service was finished the King would know how many of the fellowship had sworn to undertake the quest of the Graal, and they were counted, and found to number a hundred and fifty. They bade farewell, and mounted their horses, and rode through the streets of Camelot, and there was weeping of both rich and poor, and the King could not speak for weeping. And at sunrise they all parted company with each other, and every Knight took the way he best liked.

III

THE ADVENTURE OF SIR GALAHAD

Now Sir Galahad had as yet no shield, and he rode four days without meeting any adventure, till at last he came to a White Abbey, where he dismounted and asked if he might sleep there that night. The brethren received him with great reverence, and led him to a chamber, where he took off his armour, and then saw that he was in the presence of two Knights. 'Sirs,' said Sir Galahad, 'what adventure brought you hither?' 'Sir,' replied they, 'we heard that within this Abbey is a shield that no man may hang round his neck without being dead within three days, or some mischief befalling him. And if we fail in the adventure, you shall take it upon you.' 'Sirs,' replied Sir Galahad, 'I agree well thereto, for as yet I have no shield.'

So on the morn they arose and heard Mass, and then a monk led them behind an altar where hung a shield white as snow, with a red cross in the middle of it. 'Sirs,' said the monk, 'this shield can be hung round no Knight's neck, unless he be the worthiest Knight in the world, and therefore I counsel you to be well advised.'

'Well,' answered one of the Knights, whose name was King Bagdemagus, 'I know truly that I am not the best Knight in the world, but yet shall I try to bear it,' and he bare it out of the Abbey. Then he said to Sir Galahad, 'I pray you abide here still, till you know how I shall speed,' and he rode away, taking with him a squire to send tidings back to Sir Galahad.

After King Bagdemagus had ridden two miles he entered a fair valley, and there met him a goodly Knight seated on a white horse and clad in white armour. And they came together with their spears, and Sir Bagdemagus was borne from his horse, for the shield covered him not at all. Therewith the strange Knight alighted and took the white shield from him, and gave it to the squire, saying, 'Bear this shield to the good Knight Sir Galahad that thou hast left in the Abbey, and greet him well from me.'

'Sir,' said the squire, 'what is your name?'

'Take thou no heed of my name,' answered the Knight, 'for it is not for thee to know, nor for any earthly man.'

'Now, fair Sir,' said the squire, 'tell me for what cause this shield may not be borne lest ill befalls him who bears it.'

'Since you have asked me,' answered the Knight, 'know that no man shall bear this shield, save Sir Galahad only.'

Then the squire turned to Bagdemagus, and asked him whether he were wounded or not. 'Yes, truly,' said he, 'and I shall hardly escape from death'; and scarcely could he climb on to his horse's back when the squire brought it near him. But the squire led him to a monastery that lay in the valley, and there he was treated of his wounds, and after long lying came back to life. After the squire had given the Knight into the care of the monks, he rode back to the Abbey, bearing with him the shield. 'Sir Galahad,' said he, alighting before him, 'the Knight that wounded Bagdemagus sends you greeting, and bids you bear this shield, which shall bring you many adventures.'

'Now blessed be God and fortune,' answered Sir Galahad, and called for his arms, and mounted his horse, hanging the shield about his neck. Then, followed by the squire, he set out. They rode straight to the hermitage, where they saw the White Knight who had sent the shield to Sir Galahad. The two Knights saluted

SIR GALAHAD OPENS THE TOMB

each other courteously, and then the White Knight told Sir Galahad the story of the shield, and how it had been given into his charge. Afterwards they parted, and Sir Galahad and his squire returned unto the Abbey whence they came.

The monks made great joy at seeing Sir Galahad again, for they feared he was gone for ever ; and as soon as he was alighted from his horse they brought him unto a tomb in the churchyard where there was night and day such a noise that any man who heard it should be driven nigh mad, or else lose his strength. 'Sir,' they said, 'we deem it a fiend.' Sir Galahad drew near, all armed save his helmet, and stood by the tomb. 'Lift up the stone,' said a monk, and Galahad lifted it, and a voice cried, 'Come thou not nigh me, Sir Galahad, for thou shalt make me go again where I have been so long.' But Galahad took no heed of him, and lifted the stone yet higher, and there rushed from the tomb a foul smoke, and in the midst of it leaped out the foulest figure that ever was seen in the likeness of a man. 'Galahad,' said the figure, 'I see about thee so many angels that my power dare not touch thee.' Then Galahad, stooping down, looked into the tomb, and he saw a body all armed lying there, with a sword by his side. 'Fair brother,' said Galahad, 'let us remove this body, for he is not worthy to be in this churchyard, being a false Christian man.'

This being done they all departed and returned unto the monastery, where they lay that night, and the next morning Sir Galahad knighted Melias his squire, as he had promised him aforetime. So Sir Galahad and Sir Melias departed thence, in quest of the Holy Graal, but they soon went their different ways and fell upon different adventures. In his first encounter Sir Melias was sore wounded, and Sir Galahad came to his help, and left him to an old monk who said that he would heal him of his wounds in the space of seven weeks, and that he was

thus wounded because he had not come clean to the quest
of the Graal, as Sir Galahad had done.   Sir Galahad left
him there, and rode on till he came to the Castle of
Maidens, which he alone might enter who was free from
sin.   There he chased away the Knights who had seized
the castle seven years agone, and restored all to the
Duke's daughter, who owned it of right.   Besides this
he set free the maidens who were kept in prison, and
summoned all those Knights in the country round who
had held their lands of the Duke, bidding them do
homage to his daughter.   And in the morning one came
to him and told him that as the seven Knights fled from
the Castle of Maidens they fell upon the path of Sir
Gawaine, Sir Gareth, and Sir Lewaine, who were seeking
Sir Galahad, and they gave battle; and the seven Knights
were slain by the three Knights.   'It is well,' said Galahad, and he took his armour and his horse and rode
away.

So when Sir Galahad left the Castle of Maidens he
rode till he came to a waste forest, and there he met with
Sir Lancelot and Sir Percivale; but they knew him not,
for he was now disguised.   And they fought together,
and the two Knights were smitten down out of the
saddle.   'God be with thee, thou best Knight in the world,'
cried a nun who dwelt in a hermitage close by; and she
said it in a loud voice, so that Lancelot and Percivale
might hear.   But Sir Galahad feared that she would
make known who he was, so he spurred his horse and
struck deep into the forest before Sir Lancelot and Sir
Percivale could mount again.   They knew not which
path he had taken, so Sir Percivale turned back to ask
advice of the nun, and Sir Lancelot pressed forward.

IV

HOW SIR LANCELOT SAW A VISION, AND REPENTED OF HIS SINS

He halted when he came to a stone cross, which had by it a block of marble, while nigh at hand stood an old chapel. He tied his horse to a tree, and hung his shield on a branch, and looked into the chapel, for the door was waste and broken. And he saw there a fair altar covered with a silken cloth, and a candlestick which had six branches, all of shining silver. A great light streamed from it, and at this sight Sir Lancelot would fain have entered in, but he could not. So he turned back sorrowful and dismayed, and took the saddle and bridle off his horse, and let him pasture where he would, while he himself unlaced his helm, and ungirded his sword, and lay down to sleep upon his shield, at the foot of the cross.

As he lay there, half waking and half sleeping, he saw two white palfreys come by, drawing a litter, wherein lay a sick Knight. When they reached the cross they paused, and Sir Lancelot heard the Knight say, ' O sweet Lord, when shall this sorrow leave me, and when shall the Holy Vessel come by me, through which I shall be blessed ? For I have endured long, though my ill deeds were few.' Thus he spoke, and Sir Lancelot heard it, and of a sudden the great candlestick stood before the cross, though no man had brought it. And with it was a table of silver and the Holy Vessel of the Graal, which Lancelot had seen aforetime. Then the Knight rose up, and on his hands and knees he approached the Holy Vessel, and prayed, and was made whole of his sickness. After that the Graal went back into the chapel, and the light and the candlestick also, and Sir Lancelot would fain have followed, but could not, so heavy was the weight of his sins upon him. And the sick Knight arose and kissed the cross, and saw Sir Lancelot lying at the foot with his eyes shut. 'I marvel greatly at this sleeping Knight,' he said to his squire, 'that he had no power to wake when the Holy Vessel was brought hither.' 'I dare right well say,' answered the squire, 'that he dwelleth in some deadly sin, whereof he was never confessed.' 'By my faith,' said the Knight, 'he is unhappy, whoever he is, for he is of the fellowship of the Round Table, which have undertaken the quest of the Graal.' 'Sir,' replied the squire, 'you have all your arms here, save only your sword and your helm. Take therefore those of this strange Knight, who has just put them off.' And the Knight did as his squire said, and took Sir Lancelot's horse also, for it was better than his own.

After they had gone Sir Lancelot waked up wholly, and thought of what he had seen, wondering if he were in a dream or not. Suddenly a voice spoke to him, and it said, 'Sir Lancelot, more hard than is the stone, more bitter than is the wood, more naked and barren than is the leaf of the fig tree, art thou; therefore go from hence and withdraw thee from this holy place.' When Sir Lancelot heard this, his heart was passing heavy, and he wept, cursing the day when he had been born. But his helm and sword had gone from the spot where he had lain them at the foot of the cross, and his horse was gone also. And he smote himself and cried, 'My sin and my wickedness have done me this dishonour; for when I sought worldly adventures for worldly desires I ever achieved them and had the better in every place, and never was I discomfited in any quarrel, were it right or wrong.

1901 LANCELOT AT THE CHAPEL H.J.FORD

And now I take upon me the adventures of holy things, I see and understand that my old sin hinders me, so that I could not move nor speak when the Holy Graal passed by.' Thus he sorrowed till it was day, and he heard the birds sing, and at that he felt comforted. And as his horse was gone also, he departed on foot with a heavy heart.

V

THE ADVENTURE OF SIR PERCIVALE

All this while Sir Percivale had pursued adventures of his own, and came nigh unto losing his life, but he was saved from his enemies by the good Knight, Sir Galahad, whom he did not know, although he was seeking him, for Sir Galahad now bore a red shield, and not a white one. And at last the foes fled deep into the forest, and Sir Galahad followed; but Sir Percivale had no horse and was forced to stay behind. Then his eyes were opened, and he knew it was Sir Galahad who had come to his help, and he sat down under a tree and grieved sore.

While he was sitting there a Knight passed by riding a black horse, and when he was out of sight a yeoman came pricking after as fast as he might, and, seeing Sir Percivale, asked if he had seen a Knight mounted on a black horse. ' Yes, Sir, forsooth,' answered Sir Percivale, ' why do you want to know ? ' ' Ah, Sir, that is my steed which he has taken from me, and wherever my lord shall find me, he is sure to slay me.' ' Well,' said Sir Percivale, ' thou seest that I am on foot, but had I a good horse I would soon come up with him.' ' Take my hackney,' said the yeoman, ' and do the best you can, and I shall follow you on foot to watch how you speed.' So Sir Percivale rode as fast as he might, and at last he saw that Knight, and he hailed him. The Knight turned and set his spear against Sir Percivale, and smote the hackney in the breast, so that he fell dead to the earth, and Sir Percivale fell with him ; then the Knight rode away. But Sir Percivale was mad with wrath, and cried to the Knight to return and fight with him on foot,

SIR PERCIVALE SLAYS THE SERPENT

and the Knight answered not and went on his way. When Sir Percivale saw that he would not turn, he threw himself on the ground, and cast away his helm and sword, and bemoaned himself for the most unhappy of all Knights; and there he abode the whole day, and, being faint and weary, slept till it was midnight. And at midnight he waked and saw before him a woman, who said to him right fiercely, ' Sir Percivale, what doest thou here?' 'Neither good nor great ill,' answered he. ' If thou wilt promise to do my will when I call upon you,' said she, ' I will lend you my own horse, and he shall bear thee whither thou shalt choose.' This Sir Percivale promised gladly, and the woman went and returned with a black horse, so large and well-apparelled that Sir Percivale marvelled. But he mounted him gladly, and drove in his spurs, and within an hour and less the horse bare him four days' journey hence, and would have borne him into a rough water that roared, had not Sir Percivale pulled at his bridle. The Knight stood doubting, for the water made a great noise, and he feared lest his horse could not get through it. Still, wishing greatly to pass over, he made himself ready, and signed the sign of the cross upon his forehead.

At that the fiend which had taken the shape of a horse shook off Sir Percivale and dashed into the water, crying and making great sorrow; and it seemed to him that the water burned. Then Sir Percivale knew that it was not a horse but a fiend, which would have brought him to perdition, and he gave thanks and prayed all that night long. As soon as it was day he looked about him, and saw he was in a wild mountain, girt round with the sea and filled with wild beasts. Then he rose and went into a valley, and there he saw a young serpent bring a young lion by the neck, and after that there passed a great lion, crying and roaring after the serpent, and a fierce battle began between them. Sir Percivale thought to help the lion, as he was the more natural beast of the twain, and he drew his sword and set his shield before him, and gave the serpent a deadly buffet. When the lion saw that, he made him all the cheer that a beast might make a man, and fawned about him like a spaniel, and stroked him with his paws. And about noon the lion took his little whelp, and placed him on his back, and bare him home again, and Sir Percivale, being left alone, prayed till he was comforted. But at eventide the lion returned, and couched down at his feet, and all night long he and the lion slept together.

VI

AN ADVENTURE OF SIR LANCELOT

As Lancelot went his way through the forest he met
with many hermits who dwelled therein, and had adventure
with the Knight who stole his horse and his helm, and got
them back again. And he learned from one of the hermits
that Sir Galahad was his son, and that it was he who at
the Feast of Pentecost had sat in the Siege Perilous, which
it was ordained by Merlin that none should sit in save
the best Knight in the world. All that night Sir Lancelot
abode with the hermit and laid him to rest, a hair shirt
always on his body, and it pricked him sorely, but he
bore it meekly and suffered the pain. When the day
dawned he bade the hermit farewell. As he rode he
came to a fair plain, in which was a great castle set about
with tents and pavilions of divers hues. Here were full
five hundred Knights riding on horseback, and those near
the castle were mounted on black horses with black
trappings, and they that were without were on white
horses and their trappings white. And the two sides
fought together, and Sir Lancelot looked on.

At last it seemed to him that the black Knights nearest
the castle fared the worst, so, as he ever took the part
of the weaker, he rode to their help and smote many
of the white Knights to the earth and did marvellous
deeds of arms. But always the white Knights held round
Sir Lancelot to tire him out. And as no man may endure for ever, in the end Sir Lancelot waxed so faint of
fighting that his arms would not lift themselves to deal a
stroke ; then they took him, and led him away into the
forest and made him alight from his horse and rest,
and when he was taken the fellowship of the castle

were overcome for want of him. 'Never ere now was I at tournament or jousts but I had the best,' moaned Sir Lancelot to himself, as soon as the Knights had left him and he was alone. 'But now am I shamed, and I am persuaded that I am more sinful than ever I was.' Sorrowfully he rode on till he passed a chapel, where stood a nun, who called to him and asked him his name and what he was seeking.

So he told her who he was, and what had befallen him at the tournament, and the vision that had come to him in his sleep. 'Ah, Lancelot,' said she, 'as long as you were a Knight of earthly knighthood you were the most wonderful man in the world and the most adventurous. But now, since you are set among Knights of heavenly adventures, if you were worsted at that tournament it is no marvel. For the tournament was meant for a sign, and the earthly Knights were they who were clothed in black in token of the sins of which they were not yet purged. And the white Knights were they who had chosen the way of holiness, and in them the quest has already begun. Thus you beheld both the sinners and the good men, and when you saw the sinners overcome you went to their help, as they were your fellows in boasting and pride of the world, and all that must be left in that quest. And that caused your misadventure. Now that I have warned you of your vain-glory and your pride, beware of everlasting pain, for of all earthly Knights I have pity of you, for I know well that among earthly sinful Knights you are without peer.'

VII

AN ADVENTURE OF SIR GAWAINE

Sir Gawaine rode long without meeting any adventure, and from Pentecost to Michaelmas found none that pleased him. But at Michaelmas he met Sir Ector de Maris and rejoiced greatly.

As they sat talking there appeared before them a hand showing unto the elbow covered with red samite, and holding a great candle that burned right clear; and the hand passed into the chapel and vanished, they knew not where. Then they heard a voice which said, ' Knights full of evil faith and poor belief, these two things have failed you, and therefore you may not come to the adventure of the Holy Graal.' And this same told them a holy man to whom they confessed their sins, ' for,' said he, ' you have failed in three things, charity, fasting, and truth, and have been great murderers. But sinful as Sir Lancelot was, since he went into the quest he never slew man, nor shall, till he come into Camelot again. For he has taken upon him to forsake sin. And were he not so unstable, he should be the next to achieve it, after Galahad his son. Yet shall he die an holy man, and in earthly sinful men he has no fellow.'

' Sir,' said Gawaine, ' by your words it seems that our sins will not let us labour in that quest?' ' Truly,' answered the hermit, ' there be an hundred such as you to whom it will bring naught but shame.' So Gawaine departed and followed Sir Ector, who had ridden on before.

VIII

THE ADVENTURE OF SIR BORS

When Sir Bors left Camelot on his quest he met a holy man riding on an ass, and Sir Bors saluted him. Then the good man knew him to be one of the Knights who were in quest of the Holy Graal. ' What are you ? ' said he, and Sir Bors answered, ' I am a Knight that fain would be counselled in the quest of the Graal, for he shall have much earthly worship that brings it to an end.' ' That is true,' said the good man, ' for he will be the best Knight in the world, but know well that there shall none attain it but by holiness and by confession of sin.' So they rode together till they came to the hermitage, and the good man led Sir Bors into the chapel, where he made confession of his sins, and they ate bread and drank water together. ' Now,' said the hermit, ' I pray you that you eat none other till you sit at the table where the Holy Graal shall be.' ' Sir,' answered Sir Bors, ' I agree thereto, but how know you that I shall sit there ? ' ' That know I,' said the holy man, ' but there will be but few of your fellows with you. Also instead of a shirt you shall wear this garment until you have achieved your quest,' and Sir Bors took off his clothes, and put on instead a scarlet coat. Then the good man questioned him, and marvelled to find him pure in life, and he armed him and bade him go. After this Sir Bors rode through many lands, and had many adventures, and was often sore tempted, but remembered the words of the holy man and kept his life clean of wrong. And once he had by mischance almost slain his own brother, but a voice cried, ' Flee, Bors, and touch him not,' and he hearkened and stayed his hand. And there fell between them a fiery cloud, which burned up both their shields, and they two fell to the earth in a great swoon; but when they awakened out of it Bors saw that his brother had no harm. With that the voice spoke to him saying, 'Bors, go hence and bear your brother fellowship no longer; but take your way to the

HOW SIR BORS WAS SAVED
FROM KILLING HIS BROTHER

sea, where Sir Percivale abides till you come.' Then Sir Bors prayed his brother to forgive him all he had unknowingly done, and rode straight to the sea. On the shore he found a vessel covered with white samite, and as soon as he stepped in the vessel it set sail so fast it might have been flying, and Sir Bors lay down and slept till it was day. When he waked he saw a Knight lying in the midst of the ship, all armed save for his helm, and he knew him for Sir Percivale, and welcomed him with great joy; and they told each other of their adventures and of their temptations, and had great happiness in each other's company. 'We lack nothing but Galahad, the good Knight,' Sir Percivale said.

IX

ADVENTURE OF SIR GALAHAD

Sir Galahad rested one evening at a hermitage. And while he was resting, there came a gentlewoman and asked leave of the hermit to speak with Sir Galahad, and would not be denied, though she was told he was weary and asleep. Then the hermit waked Sir Galahad and bade him rise, as a gentlewoman had great need of him, so Sir Galahad rose and asked her what she wished. 'Galahad,' said she, 'I will that you arm yourself, and mount your horse and follow me, and I will show you the highest adventure that ever any Knight saw.' And Sir Galahad bade her go, and he would follow wherever she led. In three days they reached the sea, where they found the ship where Sir Bors and Sir Percivale were lying. And the lady bade him leave his horse behind and said she would leave hers also, but their saddles and bridles they would take on board the ship. This they did, and were received with great joy by the two Knights; then the sails were spread, and the ship was driven before the wind at a marvellous pace till they reached the land of Logris, the entrance to which lies between two great rocks with a whirlpool in the middle.

Their own ship might not get safely through; but they left it and went into another ship that lay there, which had neither man nor woman in it. At the end of the ship was written these words: 'Thou man which shall enter this ship beware thou be in steadfast belief; if thou fail, I shall not help thee.' Then the gentlewoman turned and said, 'Percivale, do you know who I am?' 'No, truly,' answered he. 'I am your sister, and therefore you are the man in the world

that I most love. If you are without faith, or have
any hidden sin, beware how you enter, else you will
perish.' 'Fair sister,' answered he, 'I shall enter therein,
for if I am an untrue Knight then shall I perish.' So
they entered the ship, and it was rich and well adorned,
that they all marvelled.

In the midst of it was a fair bed, and Sir Galahad
went thereto and found on it a crown of silk, and
a sword drawn out of its sheath half a foot and
more. The sword was of divers fashions, and the
pommel of stone, wrought about with colours, and every
colour with its own virtue, and the handle was of the
ribs of two beasts. The one was the bone of a serpent,
and no hand that handles it shall ever become weary or
hurt; and the other is the bone of a fish that swims in
Euphrates, and whoso handles it shall not think on
joy or sorrow that he has had, but only on that which he
beholds before him. And no man shall grip this sword
but one that is better than other men. So first Sir Percivale stepped forward and set his hand to the sword, but
he might not grasp it. Next Sir Bors tried to seize it,
but he also failed. When Sir Galahad beheld the sword,
he saw that there was written on it, in letters of blood,
that he who tried to draw it should never fail of shame
in his body or be wounded to the death. 'By my faith,'
said Galahad, 'I would draw this sword out of its sheath,
but the offending is so great I shall not lay my hand
thereto.' 'Sir,' answered the gentlewoman, 'know that no
man can draw this sword save you alone'; and she told
him many tales of the Knights who had set their hands to
it, and of the evil things that had befallen them. And
they all begged Sir Galahad to grip the sword, as it was
ordained that he should. 'I will grip it,' said Galahad,
'to give you courage, but it belongs no more to me than it
does to you.' Then he gripped it tight with his fingers,
and the gentlewoman girt him about the middle with the
sword, and after that they left that ship and went into

another, which brought them to land, where they fell upon many strange adventures. And when they had wrought many great deeds, they departed from each other. But first Sir Percivale's sister died, being bled to death, so that another lady might live, and she prayed them to lay her body in a boat and leave the boat to go as the winds and waves carried it. And so it was done, and Sir Percivale wrote a letter telling how she had helped them in all their adventures; and he put it in her right hand, and laid her in a barge, and covered it with black silk. And the wind arose and drove it from their sight.

X

Now we must tell what happened to Sir Lancelot.

When he was come to a water called Mortoise he fell asleep, awaiting for the adventure that should be sent to him, and in his sleep a voice spoke to him, and bade him rise and take his armour, and enter the first ship he should find. So he started up and took his arms and made him ready, and on the strand he found a ship that was without sail or oar. As soon as he was within the ship, he felt himself wrapped round with a sweetness such as he had never known before, as if all that he could desire was fulfilled. And with this joy and peace about him he fell asleep. When he woke he found near him a fair bed, with a dead lady lying on it, whom he knew to be Sir Percivale's sister, and in her hand was the tale of her adventures, which Sir Lancelot took and read. For a month or more they dwelt in that ship together, and one day, when it had drifted near the shore, he heard a sound as of a horse; and when the steps came nearer he saw that a Knight was riding him. At the sight of the ship the Knight alighted and took the saddle and bridle, and entered the ship. 'You are welcome,' said Lancelot, and the Knight saluted him and said, 'What is your name? for my heart goeth out to you.'

'Truly,' answered he, 'my name is Sir Lancelot du Lake.'

'Sir,' said the new Knight, 'you are welcome, for you were the beginner of me in the world.'

'Ah,' cried Sir Lancelot, 'is it you, then, Galahad?'

'Yes, in sooth,' said he, and kneeled down and asked

Lancelot's blessing, and then took off his helm and kissed him. And there was great joy between them, and they told each other all that had befallen them since they left King Arthur's Court. Then Galahad saw the gentlewoman dead on the bed, and he knew her, and said he held her in great worship, and that she was the best maid in the world, and how it was great pity that she had come to her death. But when Lancelot heard that Galahad had won the marvellous sword he prayed that he might see it, and kissed the pommel and the hilt, and the scabbard. 'In truth,' he said, 'never did I know of adventures so wonderful and strange.' So dwelled Lancelot and Galahad in that ship for half a year, and served God daily and nightly with all their power. And after six months had gone it befell that on a Monday they drifted to the edge of the forest, where they saw a Knight with white armour bestriding one horse and holding another all white, by the bridle. And he came to the ship, and saluted the two Knights and said, 'Galahad, you have been long enough with your father, therefore leave that ship and start upon this horse, and go on the quest of the Holy Graal.' So Galahad went to his father and kissed him, saying, 'Fair sweet father, I know not if I shall see you more till I have beheld the Holy Graal.' Then they heard a voice which said, 'The one shall never see the other till the day of doom.' 'Now, Galahad,' said Lancelot, 'since we are to bid farewell for ever now, I pray to the great Father to preserve me and you both.' 'Sir,' answered Galahad, 'no prayer availeth so much as yours.'

The next day Sir Lancelot made his way back to Camelot, where he found King Arthur and Guenevere; but many of the Knights of the Round Table were slain and destroyed more than the half. All the Court was passing glad to see Sir Lancelot, and the King asked many tidings of his son Sir Galahad.

XI

HOW SIR GALAHAD FOUND THE GRAAL AND DIED OF THAT FINDING

Sir Galahad rode on till he met Sir Percivale and afterwards Sir Bors, whom they greeted most gladly, and they bare each other company. First they came to the Castle of Carbonek, where dwelled King Pelles, who welcomed them with joy, for he knew by their coming that they had fulfilled the quest of the Graal. They then departed on other adventures, and with the blood out of the Holy Lance Galahad anointed the maimed King and healed him. That same night at midnight a voice bade them arise and quit the castle, which they did, followed by three Knights of Gaul. Then Galahad prayed every one of them that if they reached King Arthur's Court, they should salute Sir Lancelot, his father, and those Knights of the Round Table that were present, and with that he left them, and Sir Bors and Sir Percivale with him. For three days they rode till they came to a shore, and found a ship awaiting them. And in the midst of it was the table of silver, and the Holy Graal which was covered with red samite. Then were their hearts right glad, and they made great reverence thereto, and Galahad prayed that at what time he asked, he might depart out of this world. So long he prayed that at length a voice said to him, 'Galahad, thou shalt have thy desire, and when thou askest the death of the body thou shalt have it, and shalt find the life of the soul.' Percivale likewise heard the voice, and besought Galahad to tell him why he asked such things. And Galahad answered, 'The other day when we saw a part of the adventures of the Holy

LANCELOT & THE DWARF.

Graal, I was in such a joy of heart that never did man feel before, and I knew well that when my body is dead my soul shall be in joy of which the other was but a shadow.'

Some time were the three Knights in that ship, till at length they saw before them the city of Sarras. Then they took from the ship the table of silver, and Sir Percivale and Sir Bors went first, and Sir Galahad followed after to the gate of the city, where sat an old man that was crooked. At the sight of the old man Sir Galahad called to him to help them carry the table, for it was heavy. 'Truly,' answered the old man, 'it is ten years since I have gone without crutches.' 'Care not for that,' said Galahad, 'but rise up and show your good will.' So he arose and found himself as whole as ever he was, and he ran to the table and held up the side next Galahad. And there was much noise in the city that a cripple was healed by three Knights newly entered in. This reached the ears of the King, who sent for the Knights and questioned them. And they told him the truth, and of the Holy Graal; but the King listened nothing to all they said, but put them into a deep hole in the prison. Even here they were not without comfort, for a vision of the Holy Graal sustained them. And at the end of a year the King lay sick and felt he should die, and he called the three Knights and asked forgiveness of the evil he had done to them, which they gave gladly. Then he died, and the whole city was afraid and knew not what to do, till while they were in counsel a voice came to them and bade them choose the youngest of the three strange Knights for their King. And they did so. After Galahad was proclaimed King, he ordered that a coffer of gold and precious stones should be made to encompass the table of silver, and every day he and the two Knights would kneel before it and make their prayers.

Now at the year's end, and on the selfsame day that Galahad had been crowned King, he arose up early and came with the two Knights to the Palace; and he saw a man in the likeness of a Bishop, encircled by a great crowd of angels, kneeling before the Holy Vessel. And he called to Galahad and said to him, ' Come forth, thou servant of Christ, and thou shalt see what thou hast much desired to see.' Then Galahad began to tremble right hard, when the flesh first beheld the things of the spirit, and he held up his hands to heaven and said, ' Lord, I thank thee, for now I see that which hath been my desire for many a day. Now, blessed Lord, I would no longer live, if it might please thee.' Then Galahad went to Percivale and kissed him, and commended him to God; and he went to Sir Bors and kissed him, and commended him to God, and said, ' Fair lord, salute me to my lord Sir Lancelot, my father, and bid him remember this unstable world.' Therewith he kneeled down before the table and made his prayers, and while he was praying his soul suddenly left the body and was carried by angels up into heaven, which the two Knights right well beheld. Also they saw come from heaven a hand, but no body behind it, and it came unto the Vessel, and took it and the spear, and bare them back to heaven. And since then no man has dared to say that he has seen the Holy Graal.

When Percivale and Bors saw Galahad lying dead they made as much sorrow as ever two men did, and the people of the country and of the city were right heavy. And they buried him as befitted their King. As soon as Galahad was buried, Sir Percivale sought a hermitage outside the city, and put on the dress of a hermit, and Sir Bors was always with him, but kept the dress that he wore at Court. When a year and two months had passed Sir Percivale died also, and was buried by the side of Galahad; and Sir Bors left that land, and after long riding came to Camelot. Then was there great joy made of him in the Court, for they had held him as dead; and the King ordered great clerks to attend him, and to write down all his adventures and those of Sir Percivale and Sir Galahad. Next, Sir Lancelot told the adventures of the Graal which he had seen, and this likewise was written and placed with the other in almonries at Salisbury. And by and by Sir Bors said to Sir Lancelot, 'Galahad your son saluteth you by me, and after you King Arthur and all the Court, and so did Sir Percivale; for I buried them with mine own hands in the City of Sarras. Also, Sir Lancelot, Galahad prayeth you to remember of this uncertain world, as you promised when you were together!' 'That is true,' said Sir Lancelot, 'and I trust his prayer may avail me.' But the prayer but little availed Sir Lancelot, for he fell to his old sins again. And now the Knights were few that survived the search for the Graal, and the evil days of Arthur began.

THE FIGHT FOR THE QUEEN

So the quest of the Holy Graal had been fulfilled, and the few Knights that had been left alive returned to the Round Table, and there was great joy in the Court. To do them honour the Queen made them a dinner; and there were four and twenty Knights present, and among them Sir Patrise of Ireland, and Sir Gawaine and his brethren, the King's nephews, which were Sir Agrawaine, Sir Gaheris, Sir Gareth, and Sir Mordred. Now it was the custom of Sir Gawaine daily at dinner and supper to eat all manner of fruit, and especially pears and apples, and this the Queen knew, and set fruit of all sorts before him. And there was present at the dinner one Sir Pinel le Savage, who hated Sir Gawaine because he and his brethren had slain Sir Lamorak du Galis, cousin to Sir Pinel; so he put poison into some of the apples, hoping that Sir Gawaine would eat one and die. But by ill fortune it befell that the good Knight Sir Patrise took a poisoned apple, and in a few moments he lay dead and stark in his seat. At this sight all the Knights leapt to their feet, but said nothing, for they bethought them that Queen Guenevere had made them the dinner, and feared that she had poisoned the fruit.

'My lady, the Queen,' said Sir Gawaine, who was the first to speak, 'this fruit was brought for me, for all know how well I love it; therefore, Madam, the shame of this ill deed is yours.' The Queen stood still, pale and trembling, but kept silence, and next spoke Sir Mador de la Porte.

'This shall not be ended so,' said he, 'for I have lost a noble Knight of my blood, and I will be avenged of the person who has wrought this evil.' And he turned to the Queen and said, 'Madam, it is you who have brought about the death of my cousin, Sir Patrise!' The Knights round listened in silence, for they too thought Sir Mador spake truth. And the Queen still said nothing, but fell to weeping bitterly, till King Arthur heard and came to look into the matter. And when they told him of their trouble his heart was heavy within him.

'Fair lords,' said the King at last, 'I grieve for this ill deed; but I cannot meddle therein, or do battle for my wife, for I have to judge justly. Sure I am that this deed is none of hers, therefore many a good Knight will stand her champion that she be not burned to death in a wrong quarrel. And, Sir Mador, hold not your head so high, but fix the day of battle, when you shall find a Knight to answer you, or else it were great shame to all my Court.'

'My gracious lord,' said Sir Mador, 'you must hold me excused. But though you are a King you are also a Knight, and must obey the laws of knighthood. Therefore I beseech your forgiveness if I declare that none of the four and twenty Knights here present will fight that battle. What say you, my lords?' Then the Knights answered that they could not hold the Queen guiltless, for as the dinner was made by her either she or her servants must have done this thing.

'Alas!' said the Queen, 'no evil was in my heart when I prepared this feast, for never have I done such foul deeds.'

'My lord the King,' cried Sir Mador, 'I require of you, as you are a just King, to fix a day that I may get ready for the fight!'

'Well,' answered the King, 'on the fifteenth day from this come on horseback to the meadow that is by Westminster. And if it happens that there be a Knight to fight with you, strike as hard as you will, God will speed the right. But if no Knight is there, then must my Queen be burned, and a fire shall be made in the meadow.'

SIR MADOR ACCUSES GUENEVERE

'I am answered,' said Sir Mador, and he and the rest of the Knights departed.

When the King and Queen were left alone he asked

her what had brought all this about. 'God help me, that
I know not,' said the Queen, 'nor how it was done.'

'Where is Sir Lancelot?' said King Arthur, looking
round. 'If he were here, he would not grudge to do
battle for you.'

'Sir,' replied the Queen, 'I know not where he is, but
his brother and his kinsmen think he is not in this
realm.'

'I grieve for that,' said the King, 'for he would soon
stop this strife. But I counsel you, ask Sir Bors, and he
will not refuse you. For well I see that none of the four
and twenty Knights who were with you at dinner will be
your champion, and none will say well of you, but men
will speak evil of you at the Court.'

'Alas!' sighed the Queen, 'I do indeed miss Sir
Lancelot, for he would soon ease my heart.'

'What ails you?' asked the King, 'that you cannot
keep Sir Lancelot at your side, for well you know that
he who Sir Lancelot fights for has the best Knight in
the world for his champion. Now go your way, and
command Sir Bors to do battle with you for Sir Lancelot's sake.' So the Queen departed from the King, and
sent for Sir Bors into her chamber, and when he came
she besought his help.

'Madam,' said he, 'what can I do? for I may not
meddle in this matter lest the Knights who were at the
dinner have me in suspicion, for I was there also. It is
now, Madam, that you miss Sir Lancelot, whom you have
driven away, as he would have done battle for you were
you right or wrong, and I wonder how for shame's
sake you can ask me, knowing how I love and honour
him.'

'Alas,' said the Queen, 'I throw myself on your grace,'
and she went down on her knees and besought Sir Bors
to have mercy on her, 'else I shall have a shameful
death, and one I have never deserved.' At that King
Arthur came in, and found her kneeling before Sir Bors.

'Madam! you do me great dishonour,' said Sir Bors, raising her up.

'Ah, gentle Knight,' cried the King, 'have mercy on my Queen, for I am sure that they speak falsely. And I require by the love of Sir Lancelot that you do battle for her instead of him.'

'My lord,' answered Sir Bors, 'you require of me the hardest thing that ever anyone asked of me, for well you know that if I fight for the Queen I shall anger all my companions of the Round Table; but I will not say nay, my lord, for Sir Lancelot's sake and for your sake! On that day I will be the Queen's champion, unless a better Knight is found to do battle for her.'

'Will you promise me this?' asked the King.

'Yes,' answered Sir Bors, 'I will not fail you nor her, unless there should come a better Knight than I, then he shall have the battle.' Then the King and Queen rejoiced greatly, and thanked Sir Bors with all their hearts.

So Sir Bors departed and rode unto Sir Lancelot, who was with the hermit Sir Brasias, and told him of this adventure. 'Ah,' said Sir Lancelot, 'this has befallen as I would have it, and therefore I pray you make ready to do battle, but delay the fight as long as you can that I may appear. For I am sure that Sir Mador is a hot Knight, and the longer he waits the more impatient he will be for the combat.'

'Sir,' answered Sir Bors, 'let me deal with him. Doubt not you shall have all your will.' And he rode away, and came again to the Court.

It was soon noised about that Sir Bors would be the Queen's champion, and many Knights were displeased with him; but there were a few who held the Queen to be innocent. Sir Bors spoke unto them all, and said, 'It were shameful, my fair lords, if we suffered the most noble Queen in the world to be disgraced openly, not only for her sake, but for the King's.' But they an-

GVENEVERE & SIR BORS

swered him: ' As for our lord King Arthur, we love him
and honour him as much as you; but as for Queen Guenevere, we love her not, for she is the destroyer of good
Knights.'

'Fair lords,' said Sir Bors, ' you shall not speak such
words, for never yet have I heard that she was the destroyer of good Knights. But at all times, as far as I
ever knew, she maintained them and gave them many
gifts. And therefore it were a shame to us all if we suffered our noble King's wife to be put to death, and I
will not suffer it. So much I will say, that the Queen is
not guilty of Sir Patrise's death; for she owed him no
ill will, and bade him and us to the dinner for no evil
purpose, which will be proved hereafter. And in any
case there was foul dealing among us.'

' We may believe your words,' said some of the Knights,
but others held that he spoke falsely.

The days passed quickly by until the evening before
the battle, when the Queen sent for Sir Bors and asked
him if he was ready to keep his promise.

'Truly, Madam,' answered he, 'I shall not fail you,
unless a better Knight than I am come to do battle for
you. Then, Madam, I am discharged of my promise.'

' Shall I tell this to my lord Arthur ? ' said the Queen.

' If it pleases you, Madam,' answered Sir Bors. So the
Queen went to the King, and told him what Sir Bors had
said, and the King bade her to be comforted, as Sir Bors
was one of the best Knights of the Round Table.

The next morning the King and Queen, and all manner
of Knights, rode into the meadow of Westminster, where
the battle was to be; and the Queen was put into the
Guard of the High Constable, and a stout iron stake was
planted, and a great fire made about it, at which the
Queen should be burned if Sir Mador de la Porte won
the fight. For it was the custom in those days that
neither fear nor favour, love nor kinship, should hinder
right judgment. Then came Sir Mador de la Porte, and

made oath before the King that the Queen had done to death his cousin Sir Patrise, and he would prove it on her Knight's body, let who would say the contrary. Sir Bors likewise made answer that Queen Guenevere had done no wrong, and that he would make good with his two hands. 'Then get you ready,' said Sir Mador. 'Sir Mador,' answered Sir Bors, 'I know you for a good Knight, but I trust to be able to withstand your malice; and I have promised King Arthur and my lady the Queen that I will do battle for her to the uttermost, unless there come forth a better Knight than I am.'

'Is that all?' asked Sir Mador; 'but you must either fight now or own that you are beaten.'

'Take your horse,' said Sir Bors, 'for I shall not tarry long,' and Sir Mador forthwith rode into the field with his shield on his shoulder, and his spear in his hand, and he went up and down crying unto King Arthur, 'Bid your champion come forth if he dare.' At that Sir Bors was ashamed, and took his horse, and rode to the end of the lists. But from a wood hard by appeared a Knight riding fast on a white horse, bearing a shield full of strange devices. When he reached Sir Bors he drew rein and said, 'Fair Knight, be not displeased, but this battle must be to a better Knight than you. For I have come a great journey to fight this fight, as I promised when I spoke with you last, and I thank you heartily for your goodwill.' So Sir Bors went to King Arthur and told him that a Knight had come who wished to do battle for the Queen. 'What Knight is he?' asked the King.

'That I know not,' said Sir Bors; 'but he made a covenant with me to be here this day, and now I am discharged,' said Sir Bors.

Then the King called to that Knight and asked him if he would fight for the Queen. 'For that purpose I came hither,' replied he, 'and therefore, Sir King, delay me no longer, for as soon as I have ended this battle I

ARTHUR AND GUENEVERE
KISS BEFORE ALL THE PEOPLE

must go hence, as I have many matters elsewhere. And I would have you know that it is a dishonour to all the Knights of the Round Table to let so noble a lady and so courteous a Queen as Queen Guenevere be shamed amongst you.'

The Knights who were standing round looked at each other at these words, and wondered much what man this was who took the battle upon him, for none knew him save Sir Bors.

'Sir,' said Sir Mador de la Porte unto the King, 'let me know the name of him with whom I have to do.' But the King answered nothing, and made a sign for the fight to begin. They rode to the end of the lists, and couched their spears and rushed together with all their force, and Sir Mador's spear broke in pieces. But the other Knight's spear held firm, and he pressed on Sir Mador's horse till it fell backward with a great fall. Sir Mador sprang from his horse, and, placing his shield before him, drew his sword, and bade his foe dismount from his horse also, and do battle with him on foot, which the unknown Knight did. For an hour they fought thus, as Sir Mador was a strong man, and had proved himself the victor in many combats. At last the Knight smote Sir Mador grovelling to his knees, and the Knight stepped forward to have struck him flat upon the ground. Therewith Sir Mador suddenly rose, and smote the Knight upon the thigh, so that the blood ran out fiercely. But when the Knight felt himself wounded, and saw his blood, he let Sir Mador rise to his feet, and then he gave him such a buffet on the helm that this time Sir Mador fell his length on the earth, and the Knight sprang to him, to unloose his helm. At this Sir Mador prayed for his life, acknowledging that he was overcome, and confessed that the Queen's innocence had been proved. 'I will only grant you your life,' said the Knight, 'if you will proclaim publicly that you have foully slandered the Queen, and that you make no

mention, on the tomb of Sir Patrise, that ever Queen
Guenevere consented to his murder.' 'All that will I
do,' said Sir Mador, and some Knights took him up, and
carried him away to heal his wounds. And the other
Knight went straight to the foot of the steps where sat
King Arthur, and there the Queen had just come, and
the King and the Queen kissed each other before all the
people. When King Arthur saw the Knight standing
there he stooped down to him and thanked him, and so
likewise did the Queen; and they prayed him to put off
his helmet, and commanded wine to be brought, and
when he unlaced his helmet to drink they knew him to
be Sir Lancelot du Lake. Then Arthur took the Queen's
hand and led her to Sir Lancelot and said, ' Sir, I give
you the most heartfelt thanks of the great deed you have
done this day for me and my Queen.'

'My lord,' answered Sir Lancelot, 'you know well that
I ought of right ever to fight your battles, and those of
my lady the Queen. For it was you who gave me the
high honour of knighthood, and that same day my lady
the Queen did me a great service, else I should have been
put to shame before all men. Because in my hastiness I
lost my sword, and my lady the Queen found it and gave
it to me when I had sore need of it. And therefore, my
lord Arthur, I promised her that day that I would be her
Knight in right or in wrong.'

'I owe you great thanks,' said the King, 'and some
time I hope to repay you.' The Queen, beholding Sir
Lancelot, wept tears of joy for her deliverance, and felt
bowed to the ground with sorrow at the thought of what
he had done for her, when she had sent him away with
unkind words. Then all the Knights of the Round Table
and his kinsmen drew near to him and welcomed him,
and there was great mirth in the Court.

THE FAIR MAID OF ASTOLAT

Soon after this it befell that the damsel of the lake, called by some Nimue and by others Vivien, wedded Sir Pelleas, and came to the Court of King Arthur. And when she heard the talk of the death of Sir Patrise and how the Queen had been accused of it, she found out by means of her magic that the tale was false, and told it openly that the Queen was innocent and that it was Sir Pinel who had poisoned the apple. Then he fled into his own country, where none might lay hands on him. So Sir Patrise was buried in the Church of Westminster, and on his tomb was written, 'Here lieth Sir Patrise of Ireland, slain by Sir Pinel le Savage, that empoisoned apples to have slain Sir Gawaine, and by misfortune Sir Patrise ate one of those apples and then suddenly he burst.' Also there was put upon the tomb that Queen Guenevere was accused of the death of Sir Patrise by Sir Mador de la Porte, and how Sir Lancelot fought with him and overcame him in battle. All this was written on the tomb.

And daily Sir Mador prayed to have the Queen's grace once more, and by means of Sir Lancelot he was forgiven. It was now the middle of the summer, and King Arthur proclaimed that in fifteen days a great tourney should be held at Camelot, which is now called Winchester, and many Knights and Kings made ready to do themselves honour. But the Queen said she would stay behind, for she was sick, and did not care for the noise and bustle of a tourney. 'It grieves me you should say that,' said the

King, 'for you will not have seen so noble a company gathered together this seven years past, save at the Whitsuntide when Galahad departed from the Court.'

'Truly,' answered the Queen, 'the sight will be grand. Nevertheless you must hold me excused, for I cannot be there.'

Sir Lancelot likewise declared that his wounds were not healed and that he could not bear himself in a tourney as he was wont to do. At this the King was wroth, that he might not have either his Queen or his best Knight with him, and he departed towards Winchester and by the way lodged in a town now called Guildford, but then Astolat. And when the King had set forth, the Queen sent for Sir Lancelot, and told him he was to blame for having excused himself from going with the King, who set such store by his company ; and Sir Lancelot said he would be ruled by her, and would ride forth next morning on his way to Winchester; 'but I should have you know,' said he, 'that at the tourney I shall be against the King and his Knights.'

'You must do as you please,' replied the Queen, 'but if you will be ruled by my counsel, you will fight on his side.'

'Madam,' said Sir Lancelot, 'I pray you not to be displeased with me. I will take the adventure as it comes,' and early next morning he rode away till at eventide he reached Astolat. He went through the town till he stopped before the house of an old Baron, Sir Bernard of Astolat, and as he dismounted from his horse, the King spied him from the gardens of the castle. 'It is well,' he said smiling to the Knights that were beside him, 'I see one man who will play his part in the jousts, and I will undertake that he will do marvels.'

'Who is that?' asked they all. 'You must wait to know that,' replied the King, and went into the castle. Meantime Sir Lancelot had entered his lodging, and the old Baron bade him welcome, but he knew not it was Sir Lancelot. 'Fair Sir,' said Sir Lancelot, 'I pray you lend me, if you can, a shield with a device which no man knows, for mine they know well.'

'Sir,' answered Sir Bernard, 'you shall have your wish, for you seem one of the goodliest Knights in the world. And, Sir, I have two sons, both but lately knighted, Sir Tirre who was wounded on the day of his knighthood, and his shield you shall have. My youngest son, Sir Lavaine, shall ride with you, if you will have his company, to the jousts. For my heart is much drawn to you, and tell me, I beseech you, what name I shall call you by.'

'You must hold me excused as to that, just now,' said Sir Lancelot, 'but if I speed well at the jousts, I will come again and tell you. But let me have Sir Lavaine with me, and lend me, as you have offered, his brother's shield.' 'This shall be done,' replied Sir Bernard.

Besides these two sons, Sir Bernard had a daughter whom everyone called The Fair Maid of Astolat, though her real name was Elaine le Blanc. And when she looked on Sir Lancelot, her love went forth to him and she could never take it back, and in the end it killed her. As soon as her father told her that Sir Lancelot was going to the tourney she besought him to wear her token in the jousts, but he was not willing. 'Fair damsel,' he said, 'if I did that, I should have done more for your love than ever I did for lady or damsel.' But then he remembered that he was to go disguised to the tourney, and because he had before never worn any manner of token of any damsel, he bethought him that, if he should take one of hers, none would know him. So he said to her, 'Fair damsel, I will wear your token on my helmet, if you will show me what it is.'

'Sir,' she answered, 'it is a red sleeve, embroidered in great pearls,' and she brought it to him. 'Never have I done so much for any damsel,' said he, and gave his own shield into her keeping, till he came again. Sir Arthur had waited three days in Astolat for some Knights

who were long on the road, and when they had arrived
they all set forth, and were followed by Sir Lancelot and
Sir Lavaine, both with white shields, and Sir Lancelot bore
besides the red sleeve that was a token.   Now Camelot
was filled with a great number of Kings and Lords and
Knights, but Sir Lavaine found means to lodge both himself and Sir Lancelot secretly with a rich burgess, and no
man knew who they were or whence they came.   And
there they stayed till the day of the tourney.   At earliest
dawn the trumpets blew, and King Arthur took his seat
upon a high scaffold, so that he might see who had done
best; but he would not suffer Sir Gawaine to go from
his side, for Sir Gawaine never won the prize when Sir
Lancelot was in the field, and as King Arthur knew, Sir
Lancelot oftentimes disguised himself.

Then the Knights formed into two parties and Sir
Lancelot made him ready, and fastened the red sleeve
upon his helmet, and he and Sir Lavaine rode into a little wood that lay behind the Knights who should fight
against those of the Round Table.   'Sir,' said Sir
Lancelot, 'yonder is a company of good Knights and
they hold together as boars that are vexed with dogs.'

'That is truth,' said Sir Lavaine.

'Now,' said Sir Lancelot, 'if you will help me a little,
you shall see King Arthur's side, which is winning, driven
back as fast as they came.'

'Spare not, Sir,' answered Sir Lavaine, 'for I shall do
what I may.'   So they rode into the thickest of the press,
and smote so hard both with spear and sword that the
Knights of the Round Table fell back.   'O mercy!' cried
Sir Gawaine, 'what Knight is that yonder who does such
marvellous deeds?'

'I know well who it is,' said King Arthur, 'but I will
not tell you yet.'

'Sir,' answered Sir Gawaine, 'I should say it was Sir
Lancelot by the blows he deals and the manner that he
rides, but it cannot be he, for this man has a red sleeve

ELAINE TIES HER SLEEVE ROVND
SIR LANCELOT'S HELMET

upon his helmet, and Sir Lancelot has never borne the token of any lady.'

'Let him be,' said Sir Arthur, 'you will find out his name, and see him do greater deeds yet, before he departs.' And the Knights that were fighting against the King's party took heart again, for before they feared they would be beaten. But when Sir Bors saw this, he called unto him the Knights that were of kin to Sir Lancelot, and they banded together to make a great charge, and threw Sir Lancelot's horse to the ground, and by misfortune the spear of Sir Bors broke, and its head was left in Sir Lancelot's side. When Sir Lavaine saw that, he unhorsed the King of Scots, and brought his horse to Sir Lancelot, and helped him mount thereon and gave him a spear, with which Sir Lancelot smote Sir Bors to the earth and Sir Ector de Maris, the foster-father of King Arthur, and buffeted sorely the Knights that were with them. Afterward he hurled himself into the thick *mêlée* of them all, and did the most wonderful deeds that ever were heard of. And Sir Lavaine likewise did well that day, for he smote down full two Knights of the Round Table. 'Mercy,' again cried Sir Gawaine to Arthur, 'I marvel what Knight that is with the red sleeve.'

'That you shall know soon,' said King Arthur, and commanded that the trumpets should be blown, and declared that the prize belonged to the Knight with the white shield, who bare the red sleeve, for he had unhorsed more than thirty Knights. And the Kings and Lords who were of his party came round him and thanked him for the help he had given them, by which means the honours of the day had been theirs.

'Fair Lords,' said Sir Lancelot, 'if I have deserved thanks, I have paid for them sorely, for I shall hardly escape with my life, therefore I pray you let me depart, for my hurt is grievous.' Then he groaned piteously, and galloped from them to a wood's side, followed by Sir Lavaine. 'Oh help me, Sir Lavaine,' said he, 'to get

this spear's head out of my side, for it is killing me.' But
Sir Lavaine feared to touch it, lest Sir Lancelot should
bleed to death. ' I charge you,' said Sir Lancelot, ' if you
love me draw out the head,' so Sir Lavaine drew it out.
And Sir Lancelot gave a great shriek, and a marvellous
grisly groan, and his blood flowed out so fast, that he fell
into a swoon. ' Oh what shall I do ? ' cried Sir Lavaine,
and he loosed Sir Lancelot's helm and coat of mail, and
turned him so that the wind might blow on him, but for
full half an hour he lay as if he had been dead. And at
last Sir Lancelot opened his eyes, and said, ' O Lavaine,
help me on my horse, for two miles from this place there
lives a hermit who once was a Knight of the Round
Table, and he can heal my wounds.' Then Sir Lavaine,
with much ado, helped him on his horse, and brought
him bleeding to the hermit. The hermit looked at him
as he rode up, leaning piteously on his saddle-bow, and
he thought that he should know him, but could not tell
who he was for the paleness of his face, till he saw by a
wound on his cheek that it was Sir Lancelot.

' You cannot hide your name from me,' said the hermit, ' for you are the noblest Knight in the world, and
well I know you to be Sir Lancelot.'

' Since you know me, Sir,' said he, ' help me for God's
sake, and for death or life put me out of this pain.'

' Fear nothing,' answered the hermit, ' your pain will
soon be gone,' and he called his servants to take the
armour off the Knight, and laid him in bed. After that
he dressed the wound, and gave him good wine to drink,
and Sir Lancelot slept and awoke free of his pain. So
we will leave him to be healed of his wound, under the
care of the hermit, and go back to King Arthur.

Now it was the custom in those days that after a
tourney was finished, a great feast should be held at
which both parties were assembled, so King Arthur sent
to ask the King of Northgalis, where was the Knight
with the red sleeve, who had fought on his side. ' Bring

him before me,' he said, 'that he may have the prize he
has won, which is his right.' Then answered the King
with the hundred Knights, 'we fear the Knight must
have been sore hurt, and that neither you nor we are
ever like to see him again, which is grievous to think of.'

'Alas!' said King Arthur, 'is he then so badly
wounded? What is his name?'

'Truly,' said they all, 'we know not his name, nor
whence he came, nor whither he went.'

'As for me,' answered King Arthur, 'these tidings are
the worst that I have heard these seven years, for I would
give all the lands I hold that no harm had befallen this
Knight.'

'Do you know him?' asked they all.

'Whether I know him or not,' said King Arthur, 'I
shall not tell you, but may Heaven send me good news
of him.' 'Amen,' answered they.

'By my head,' said Sir Gawaine, 'if this good Knight
is really wounded unto death, it is a great evil for all this
land, for he is one of the noblest that ever I saw for
handling a sword or spear. And if he may be found, I
shall find him, for I am sure he is not far from this town,'
so he took his squire with him, and they rode all round
Camelot, six or seven miles on every side, but nothing
could they hear of him. And he returned heavily to the
Court of King Arthur.

Two days after the King and all his company set out
for London, and by the way, it happened to Sir Gawaine
to lodge with Sir Bernard at Astolat. And when he was
in his chamber, Sir Bernard and his daughter Elaine
came unto Sir Gawaine, to ask him tidings of the Court,
and who did best in the tourney at Winchester.

'Truly,' said Sir Gawaine, 'there were two Knights
that bare white shields, but one of them had a red sleeve
upon his helm, and he was one of the best Knights that
ever I saw joust in the field, for I dare say he smote down
forty Knights of the Table Round.'

'Now blessed be God,' said the Maid of Astolat, 'that that Knight sped so well, for he is the man in the world that I loved first, and he will also be the last that ever I shall love.'

'Fair maid,' asked Sir Gawaine, 'is that Knight your love?'

'Certainly he is my love,' said she.

'Then you know his name?' asked Sir Gawaine.

'Nay, truly,' answered the damsel, 'I know neither his name, nor whence he cometh, but I love him for all that.'

'How did you meet him first?' asked Sir Gawaine. At that she told him the whole story, and how her brother went with Sir Lancelot to do him service, and lent him the white shield of her brother Sir Tirre and left his own shield with her. 'Why did he do that?' asked Sir Gawaine.

'For this cause,' said the damsel, 'his shield was too well known among many noble Knights.'

'Ah, fair damsel,' said Sir Gawaine, 'I beg of you to let me have a sight of that shield.'

'Sir,' answered she, 'it is in my chamber covered with a case, and if you will come with me, you shall see it.'

'Not so,' said Sir Bernard, and sent his squire for it. And when Sir Gawaine took off the case and beheld the shield, and saw the arms, he knew it to be Sir Lancelot's. 'Ah mercy,' cried he, 'my heart is heavier than ever it was before!'

'Why?' asked Elaine.

'I have great cause,' answered Sir Gawaine. 'Is that Knight who owns this shield your love?'

'Yes, truly,' said she; 'I would I were his love.'

'You are right, fair damsel,' replied Gawaine, 'for if you love him, you love the most honourable Knight in the world. I have known him for four-and-twenty years, and never did I or any other Knight see him wear a token of either lady or damsel at a tournament. Therefore, damsel, he has paid you great honour. But I fear that I may never behold him again upon earth, and that is grievous to think of.'

'Alas!' she said, 'how may this be? Is he slain?'

'I did not say that,' replied Sir Gawaine, 'but he is sorely wounded, and is more likely to be dead than alive. And, maiden, by this shield I know that he is Sir Lancelot.'

'How can this be?' said the Maid of Astolat, 'and what was his hurt?'

'Truly,' answered Sir Gawaine, 'it was the man that loved him best who hurt him so, and I am sure that if that man knew that it was Sir Lancelot whom he had wounded, he would think it was the darkest deed that ever he did.'

'Now, dear father,' said Elaine, 'give me leave to ride and to seek him, for I shall go out of my mind unless I find him and my brother.'

'Do as you will,' answered her father, 'for I am grieved to hear of the hurt of that noble Knight.' So the damsel made ready.

On the morn Sir Gawaine came to King Arthur and told him how he had found the shield in the keeping of the Maid of Astolat. 'All that I knew beforehand,' said the King, ' and that was why I would not suffer you to fight at the tourney, for I had espied him when he entered his lodging the night before. But this is the first time that ever I heard of his bearing the token of some lady, and much I marvel at it.'

'By my head,' answered Sir Gawaine, 'the Fair Maiden of Astolat loves him wondrous well. What it all means, or what will be the end, I cannot say, but she has ridden after him to seek him.' So the King and his company came to London, and everyone in the Court knew that it was Sir Lancelot who had jousted the best.

And when the tidings came to Sir Bors, his heart grew

heavy, and also the hearts of his kinsmen. But when
the Queen heard that Sir Lancelot bore the red sleeve of
the Fair Maid of Astolat, she was nearly mad with wrath,
and summoned Sir Bors before her in haste.

'Ah, Sir Bors,' she cried when he was come, 'have the
tidings reached you that Sir Lancelot has been a false
Knight to me ?'

'Madam,' answered Sir Bors, 'I pray you say not so,
for I cannot hear such language of him.'

'Why, is he not false and a traitor when, after swear-
ing that for right or wrong he would be my Knight and
mine only, he bore the red sleeve upon his helm at the
great jousts at Camelot ?'

'Madam,' said Sir Bors, 'I grieve bitterly as to that
sleeve-bearing, but I think he did it that none of his kin
should know him.   For no man before that had seen him
bear the token of any lady, be she what she may.'

'Fie on him !' said the Queen, 'I myself heard Sir
Gawaine tell my lord Arthur of the great love that is
between the Fair Maiden of Astolat and him.'

'Madam,' answered Sir Bors, 'I cannot hinder Sir
Gawaine from saying what he pleases, but as for Sir
Lancelot, I am sure that he loves no one lady or maiden
better than another.   And therefore I will hasten to seek
him wherever he be.'

Meanwhile fair Elaine came to Winchester to find Sir
Lancelot, who lay in peril of his life in the hermit's dwelling.   And when she was riding hither and thither, not
knowing where she should turn, she fell on her brother
Sir Lavaine, who was exercising his horse.   'How doth
my lord Sir Lancelot ?' asked she.

'Who told you, sister, that my lord's name was Sir
Lancelot ?' answered Sir Lavaine.

'Sir Gawaine, who came to my father's house to rest
after the tourney, knew him by his shield,' said she, and
they rode on till they reached the hermitage, and Sir
Lavaine brought her to Sir Lancelot.   And when she saw

him so pale, and in such a plight, she fell to the earth in
a swoon, but by-and-bye she opened her eyes and said,
'My lord Sir Lancelot, what has brought you to this?'
and swooned again. When she came to herself and stood
up, Sir Lancelot prayed her to be of good cheer, for if she
had come to comfort him she was right welcome, and
that his wound would soon heal. 'But I marvel,' said
he, 'how you know my name.' Then the maiden told
him how Sir Gawaine had been at Astolat and had seen
his shield.

'Alas!' sighed Sir Lancelot, 'it grieves me that my
name is known, for trouble will come of it.' For he
knew full well that Sir Gawaine would tell Queen
Guenevere, and that she would be wroth. And Elaine
stayed and tended him, and Sir Lancelot begged Sir
Lavaine to ride to Winchester and ask if Sir Bors was
there, and said that he should know him by token of a
wound which Sir Bors had on his forehead. 'For well I
am sure,' said Sir Lancelot, 'that Sir Bors will seek me,
as he is the same good Knight that hurt me.'

Therefore as Sir Lancelot commanded, Sir Lavaine
rode to Winchester and inquired if Sir Bors had been
seen there, so that when he entered the town Sir Lavaine
readily found him. Sir Bors was overjoyed to hear good
tidings of Sir Lancelot, and they rode back together to
the hermitage. At the sight of Sir Lancelot lying in his
bed, pale and thin, Sir Bors' heart gave way, and he
wept long without speaking. 'Oh, my lord Sir Lancelot,'
he said at last, 'God send you hasty recovery; great is
my shame for having wounded you thus, you who are
the noblest Knight in the world. I wonder that my arm
would lift itself against you, and I ask your mercy.'

'Fair cousin,' answered Sir Lancelot, 'such words
please me not at all, for it is the fault of my pride which
would overcome you all, that I lie here to-day. We will
not speak of it any more, for what is done cannot be
undone, but let us find a cure so that I may soon be

whole.' Then Sir Bors leaned upon his bed, and told
him how the Queen was filled with anger against him,
because he wore the red sleeve at the jousts.

'I am sorrowful at what you tell me,' replied Sir
Lancelot, 'for all I did was to hinder my being known.'

'That I said to excuse you,' answered Sir Bors,
'though it was all in vain. But is this damsel that is so
busy about you the Fair Maid of Astolat?'

'She it is, and she will not go from me!'

'Why should she go from you?' asked Sir Bors.
'She is a passing fair damsel, and of gentle breeding, and
I would that you could love her, for it is easy to see by
her bearing that she loves you entirely.'

'It grieves me to hear that,' said Sir Lancelot.

After this they talked of other things, till in a few
days Sir Lancelot's wounds were whole again. When
Sir Lancelot felt his strength return, Sir Bors made him
ready, and departed for the Court of King Arthur, and
told them how he had left Sir Lancelot. And there was
on All Hallows a great tournament, and Sir Bors won
the prize for the unhorsing of twenty Knights, and Sir
Gareth did great deeds also, but vanished suddenly from
the field, and no man knew where he had gone. After
the tourney was over, Sir Bors rode to the hermitage to
see Sir Lancelot, whom he found walking on his feet, and
on the next morning they bade farewell to the hermit,
taking with them Elaine le Blanc. They went first to
Astolat, where they were well lodged in the house of Sir
Bernard, but when the morrow came, and Sir Lancelot
would have departed from them, Elaine called to her father
and to her brothers Sir Tirre and Sir Lavaine, and thus
she said:

'My lord Sir Lancelot, fair Knight, leave me not, I
pray you, but have mercy upon me, and suffer me not to
die of love of thee.'

'What do you wish me to do?' asked Sir Lancelot.

'I would have you for my husband,' answered she.

'Fair damsel, I thank you,' said Sir Lancelot, 'but truly I shall never have a wife. But in token and thanks of all your good will towards me, gladly will I give a thousand pounds yearly when you set your heart upon some other Knight.'

'Of such gifts I will have none,' answered Elaine, 'and I would have you know, Sir Lancelot, that if you refuse to wed me, my good days are done.'

'Fair damsel,' said Sir Lancelot, 'I cannot do the thing that you ask.'

At these words she fell down in a swoon, and her maids bore her to her chamber, where she made bitter sorrow. Sir Lancelot thought it would be well for him to depart before she came to her senses again, and he asked Sir Lavaine what he would do.

'What should I do?' asked Sir Lavaine, 'but follow you if you will have me.' Then Sir Bernard came and said to Sir Lancelot, 'I see well that my daughter Elaine will die for your sake.'

'I cannot marry her,' answered Sir Lancelot, 'and it grieves me sorely, for she is a good maiden, fair and gentle.'

'Father,' said Sir Lavaine, 'she is as pure and good as Sir Lancelot has said, and she is like me, for since first I saw him I can never leave him.' And after that they bade the old man farewell and came unto Winchester, where the King and all the Knights of the Round Table made great joy of him, save only Sir Agrawaine and Sir Mordred. But the Queen was angry and would not speak to him, though he tried by all means to make her. Now when the Fair Maid of Astolat knew he was gone, she would neither eat nor sleep, but cried after Sir Lancelot all the day long. And when she had spent ten days in this manner, she grew so weak that they thought her soul must quit this world, and the priest came to her, and bade her dwell no more on earthly things. She would not listen to him, but cried ever after

Sir Lancelot, and how she had loved none other, no, nor ever would, and that her love would be her death. Then she called her father, Sir Bernard, and her brother, Sir Tirre, and begged her brother to write her a letter as she should tell him, and her father that he would have her watched till she was dead. 'And while my body is warm,' said she, 'let this letter be put in my right hand, and my hand bound fast with the letter until I be cold, and let me be dressed in my richest clothes and be lain on a fair bed, and driven in a chariot to the Thames. There let me be put on a barge, and a dumb man with me, to steer the barge, which shall be covered over with black samite. Thus, father, I beseech you, let it be done.' And her father promised her faithfully that so it should be done to her when she was dead. Next day she died, and her body was lain on the bed, and placed in a chariot, and driven to the Thames, where the man awaited her with the barge. When she was put on board, he steered the barge to Westminster and rowed a great while to and fro, before any espied it. At last King Arthur and Queen Guenevere withdrew into a window to speak together, and espied the black barge, and wondered greatly what it meant. The King summoned Sir Kay, and bade him take Sir Brandiles and Sir Agrawaine, and find out who was lying there, and they ran down to the river side, and came and told the King. 'That fair corpse will I see,' returned the King, and he took the Queen's hand and led her thither. Then he ordered the barge to be made fast, and he entered it, and the Queen likewise, and certain Knights with them. And there he saw a fair woman on a rich bed, and her clothing was of cloth of gold, and she lay smiling. While they looked, all being silent, the Queen spied a letter in her right hand, and pointed it out to the King, who took it saying, 'Now I am sure this letter will tell us what she was, and why she came hither.' So leaving the barge in charge of a trusty man, they went into the King's chamber, followed by many

THE BLACK BARGET

Knights, for the King would have the letter read openly.
He then broke the seal himself, and bade a clerk read it,
and this was what it said:

'Most noble Knight Sir Lancelot, I was your lover,
whom men called the Fair Maid of Astolat: therefore
unto all ladies I make my moan; yet pray for my soul,
and bury me. This is my last request. Pray for my
soul, Sir Lancelot, as thou art peerless.'

This was all the letter, and the King and Queen and
all the Knights wept when they heard it.

'Let Sir Lancelot be sent for,' presently said the King,
and when Sir Lancelot came the letter was read to him
also.

'My lord Arthur,' said he, after he had heard it all,
'I am right grieved at the death of this damsel. God
knows I was not, of my own will, guilty of her death,
and that I will call on her brother, Sir Lavaine, to
witness. She was both fair and good, and much was I
beholden to her, but she loved me out of measure.'

'You might have been a little gentle with her,'
answered the Queen, 'and have found some way to save
her life.'

'Madam,' said Sir Lancelot, 'she would have nothing
but my love, and that I could not give her, though I
offered her a thousand pounds yearly if she should set
her heart on any other Knight. For, Madam, I love not
to be forced to love; love must arise of itself, and not by
command.'

'That is truth,' replied the King, 'love is free in himself, and never will be bounden; for where he is bounden
he looseth himself. But, Sir Lancelot, be it your care to
see that the damsel is buried as is fitting.'

LANCELOT AND GUENEVERE

Now we come to the sorrowful tale of Lancelot and Guenevere, and of the death of King Arthur. Already it has been told that King Arthur had wedded Guenevere, the daughter of Leodegrance, King of Cornwall, a damsel who seemed made of all the flowers, so fair was she, and slender, and brilliant to look upon. And the Knights in her father's Court bowed down before her, and smote their hardest in the jousts where Guenevere was present, but none dared ask her in marriage till Arthur came. Like the rest he saw and loved her, but, unlike them, he was a King, and might lift his eyes even unto Guenevere. The maiden herself scarcely saw or spoke to him, but did her father's bidding in all things, and when he desired her to make everything ready to go clothed as beseemed a Princess to King Arthur's Court, her heart beat with joy at the sight of rich stuffs and shining jewels. Then one day there rode up to the Castle a band of horsemen sent by the King to bring her to his Court, and at the head of them Sir Lancelot du Lake, friend of King Arthur, and winner of all the jousts and tourna-ments where Knights meet to gain honour. Day by day they rode together apart and he told her tales of gallant deeds done for love of beautiful ladies, and they passed under trees gay with the first green of spring, and over hyacinths covering the earth with sheets of blue, till at sunset they drew rein before the silken pavilion, with the banner of Uther Pendragon floating on the top. And Guenevere's heart went out to Lancelot before she knew.

132

LANCELOT · BRINGS · GUENEVERE · TO · ARTHUR

One evening she noted, far across the plain, towers and buildings shining in the sun, and an array of horsemen ride forth to meet her. One stopped before her dazzled eyes, and leaping from his horse bowed low. Arthur had come to welcome her, and do her honour, and to lead her home. But looking up at him, she thought him cold, and, timid and alone, her thoughts turned again to Lancelot. After that the days and years slipped by, and these two were ever nearest the King, and in every time of danger the King cried for Lancelot, and trusted his honour and the Queen's to him. Sir Lancelot spoke truly when he told Elaine that he had never worn the badge of lady or maiden, but for all that every one looked on Sir Lancelot as the Queen's Knight, who could do no worship to any other woman. The King likewise held Sir Lancelot bound to fight the Queen's battles, and if he was absent on adventures of his own, messengers hastened to bring him back, as in the fight with Sir Mador. So things went on for many years, and the King never guessed that the Queen loved Lancelot best.

It befell one spring, in the month of May, that Queen Guenevere bethought herself that she would like to go a-maying in the woods and fields that lay round the City of Westminster on both sides of the river. To this intent she called her own especial Knights, and bade them be ready the next morning clothed all in green, whether of silk or cloth, 'and,' said she, 'I shall bring with me ten ladies, and every Knight shall have a lady behind him, and be followed by a squire and two yeomen, and I will that you shall all be well horsed.' Thus it was done, and the ten Knights, arrayed in fresh green, the emblem of the spring, rode with the Queen and her ladies in the early dawn, and smelt the sweet of the year, and gathered flowers which they stuck in their girdles and doublets. The Queen was as happy and light of heart as the youngest maiden, but she had promised to be with the King at the hour of ten, and gave the signal for

departure unwillingly.   The Knights were mounting
their horses, when suddenly out of a wood on the other
side rode Sir Meliagraunce, who for many years had
loved the Queen, and had sought an occasion to carry
her off, but found none so fair as this.   Out of the forest
he rode, with two score men in armour, and a hundred
archers behind him, and bade the Queen and her followers stay where they were, or they would fare badly.
'Traitor,' cried the Queen, 'what evil deed would you do?
You are a King's son and a Knight of the Round Table,
yet you seek to shame the man who gave you knighthood.   But I tell you that you may bring dishonour on
yourself, but you will bring none on me, for rather would
I cut my throat in twain.'

'As for your threats, Madam, I pay them no heed,'
returned Sir Meliagraunce; 'I have loved you many a
year, and never could I get you at such an advantage as
I do now, and therefore I will take you as I find you.'
Then all the Knights spoke together saying, 'Sir Meliagraunce, bethink yourself that in attacking men who are
unarmed you put not only our lives in peril but your
own honour.   Rather than allow the Queen to be
shamed we will each one fight to the death, and if we
did aught else we should dishonour our knighthood for
ever.'

'Fight as well as you can,' answered Sir Meliagraunce,
'and keep the Queen if you may.'   So the Knights of
the Round Table drew their swords, and the men of Sir
Meliagraunce ran at them with spears; but the Knights
stood fast, and clove the spears in two before they
touched them.   Then both sides fought with swords, and
Sir Kay and five other Knights were felled to the ground
with wounds all over their bodies.   The other four fought
long, and slew forty of the men and archers of Sir
Meliagraunce; but in the end they too were overcome.
When the Queen saw that she cried out for pity and
sorrow, 'Sir Meliagraunce, spare my noble Knights and

I will go with you quietly on this condition, that their lives be saved, and that wherever you may carry me they shall follow. For I give you warning that I would rather slay myself than go with you without my Knights, whose duty it is to guard me.'

'Madam,' replied Sir Meliagraunce, 'for your sake they shall be led with you into my own castle, if you will consent to ride with me.' So the Queen prayed the four Knights to fight no more, and she and they would not part, and to this, though their hearts were heavy, they agreed.

The fight being ended the wounded Knights were placed on horseback, some sitting, some lying across the saddle, according as they were hurt, and Sir Meliagraunce forbade anyone to leave the castle (which had been a gift to him from King Arthur), for sore he dreaded the vengeance of Sir Lancelot if this thing should reach his ears. But the Queen knew well what was passing in his mind, and she called a little page who served her in her chamber and desired him to take her ring and hasten with all speed to Sir Lancelot, 'and pray him, if he loves me, to rescue me. Spare not your horse, neither for water nor for land.' And the boy bided his time, then mounted his horse, and rode away as fast as he might. Sir Meliagraunce spied him as he flew, and knew whither he went, and who had sent him; and he commanded his best archers to ride after him and shoot him ere he reached Sir Lancelot. But the boy escaped their arrows, and vanished from their sight. Then Sir Meliagraunce said to the Queen, 'You seek to betray me, Madam; but Sir Lancelot shall not so lightly come at you.' And he bade his men follow him to the castle in haste, and left an ambush of thirty archers in the road, charging them that if a Knight mounted on a white horse came along that way they were to slay the horse but to leave the man alone, as he was hard to overcome. After Sir Meliagraunce had given these orders his company galloped fast to the castle; but the Queen would

listen to nothing that he said, demanding always that
her Knights and ladies should be lodged with her, and
Sir Meliagraunce was forced to let her have her will.

GUENEVERE SENDS HER PAGE TO LANCELOT FOR HELP

The castle of Sir Meliagraunce was distant seven miles from Westminster, so it did not take long for the boy to find Sir Lancelot, and to give him the Queen's ring and her message. 'I am shamed for ever,' said Sir Lancelot, 'unless I can rescue that noble lady,' and while he put on his armour, he called to the boy to tell him the whole adventure. When he was armed and mounted, he begged the page to warn Sir Lavaine where he had gone, and for what cause. 'And pray him, as he loves me, that he follow me to the castle of Sir Meliagraunce, for if I am a living man, he will find me there.'

Sir Lancelot put his horse into the water at Westminster, and he swam straight over to Lambeth, and soon after he landed he found traces of the fight. He rode along the track till he came to the wood, where the archers were lying waiting for him, and when they saw him, they bade him on peril of his life to go no further along that path.

'Why should I, who am a Knight of the Round Table, turn out of any path that pleases me?' asked Sir Lancelot.

'Either you will leave this path or your horse will be slain,' answered the archers.

'You may slay my horse if you will,' said Sir Lancelot, 'but when my horse is slain I shall fight you on foot, and so would I do, if there were five hundred more of you.' With that they smote the horse with their arrows, but Sir Lancelot jumped off, and ran into the wood, and they could not catch him. He went on some way, but the ground was rough, and his armour was heavy, and sore he dreaded the treason of Sir Meliagraunce. His heart was near to fail him, when there passed by a cart with two carters that came to fetch wood. 'Tell me, carter,' asked Sir Lancelot, 'what will you take to suffer me to go in your cart till we are within two miles of the castle of Sir Meliagraunce?'

'I cannot take you at all,' answered the carter, 'for I am come to fetch wood for my lord Sir Meliagraunce.'

'It is with him that I would speak.'

'You shall not go with me,' said the carter, but hardly had he uttered the words when Sir Lancelot leapt up into the cart, and gave him such a buffet that he fell dead on the ground. At this sight the other carter cried that he would take the Knight where he would if he would only spare his life. 'Then I charge you,' said Sir Lancelot, 'that you bring me to the castle gate.' So the carter drove at a great gallop, and Sir Lancelot's horse, who had espied his master, followed the cart, though more than fifty arrows were standing in his body. In an hour and a half they reached the castle gate, and were seen of Guenevere and her ladies, who were standing in a window. 'Look, Madam,' cried one of her ladies, 'in that cart yonder is a goodly armed Knight. I suppose he is going to his hanging.'

'Where?' asked the Queen, and as she spoke she espied that it was Sir Lancelot, and that his horse was following riderless. 'Well is he that has a trusty friend,' said she, 'for a noble Knight is hard pressed when he rides in a cart,' and she rebuked the lady who had declared he was going to his hanging. 'It was foul talking, to liken the noblest Knight in the world to one going to a shameful death.' By this Sir Lancelot had come to the gate of the castle, and he got down and called till the castle rang with his voice. 'Where is that false traitor Sir Meliagraunce, Knight of the Round Table? Come forth, you and your company, for I, Sir Lancelot du Lake, am here to do battle with you.' Then he burst the gate open wide, and smote the porter who tried to hold it against him. When Sir Meliagraunce heard Sir Lancelot's voice, he ran into Queen Guenevere's chamber, and fell on his knees before her: 'Mercy, Madam, mercy! I throw myself upon your grace.'

What ails you now?' said she; 'of a truth I might

THE ARCHERS THREATEN LANCELOT

well expect some good Knight to avenge me, though my lord Arthur knew not of your work.'

'Madam, I will make such amends as you yourself may desire,' pleaded Sir Meliagraunce, 'and I trust wholly to your grace.'

'What would you have me do?' asked the Queen.

'Rule in this castle as if it were your own, and give Sir Lancelot cheer till to-morrow, and then you shall all return to Westminster.'

'You say well,' answered the Queen. 'Peace is ever better than war, and I take no pleasure in fighting.' So she went down with her ladies to Sir Lancelot, who still stood full of rage in the inner court, calling as before, 'Traitor Knight, come forth!'

'Sir Lancelot,' asked the Queen, 'what is the cause of all this wrath?'

'Madam,' replied Sir Lancelot, 'does such a question come from you? Methinks your wrath should be greater than mine, for all the hurt and the dishonour have fallen upon you. My own hurt is but little, but the shame is worse than any hurt.'

'You say truly,' replied the Queen, 'but you must come in with me peaceably, as all is put into my hand, and the Knight repents bitterly of his adventure.'

'Madam,' said Sir Lancelot, 'since you have made agreement with him, it is not my part to say nay, although Sir Meliagraunce has borne himself both shamefully and cowardly towards me. But had I known you would have pardoned him so soon, I should not have made such haste to come to you.'

'Why do you say that?' asked the Queen; 'do you repent yourself of your good deeds? I only made peace with him to have done with all this noise of slanderous talk, and for the sake of my Knights.'

'Madam,' answered Sir Lancelot, 'you understand full well that I was never glad of slander nor noise, but there is neither King, Queen nor Knight alive, save yourself, Madam, and my lord Arthur, that should hinder me from giving Sir Meliagraunce a cold heart before I departed hence.'

'That I know well,' said the Queen, 'but what would you have more? Everything shall be ordered as you will.'

'Madam,' replied Sir Lancelot, 'as long as you are pleased, that is all I care for,' so the Queen led Sir Lancelot into her chamber, and commanded him to take off his armour, and then took him to where her ten Knights were lying sore wounded. And their souls leapt with joy when they saw him, and he told them how falsely Sir Meliagraunce had dealt with him, and had set archers to slay his horse, so that he was fain to place himself in a cart. Thus they complained each to the other, and would have avenged themselves on Sir Meliagraunce but for the peace made by the Queen. And in the evening came Sir Lavaine, riding in great haste, and Sir Lancelot was glad that he was come.

Now Sir Lancelot was right when he feared to trust Sir Meliagraunce, for that Knight only sought to work ill both to him and to the Queen, for all his fair words. And first he began to speak evil of the Queen to Sir Lancelot, who dared him to prove his foul words, and it was settled between them that a combat should take place in eight days in the field near Westminster. 'And now,' said Sir Meliagraunce, 'since it is decided that we must fight together, I beseech you, as you are a noble Knight, do me no treason nor villainy in the meantime.'

'Any Knight will bear me witness,' answered Sir Lancelot, 'that never have I broken faith with any man, nor borne fellowship with those that have done so.' 'Then let us go to dinner,' said Sir Meliagraunce, 'and afterwards you may all ride to Westminster. Meanwhile would it please you to see the inside of this castle?' 'That I will gladly,' said Sir Lancelot, and they went from chamber to chamber, till they reached the floor of the castle, and as he went Sir Lancelot trod on a trap, and the board rolled, and he fell down in a cave which was filled with straw, and Sir Meliagraunce departed and no man knew where Sir Lancelot might be. The Queen bethought herself that he was wont to disappear suddenly, and as Sir Meliagraunce had first removed Sir Lavaine's horse from the place where it had been tethered, the Knights agreed with her. So time passed till dinner had been eaten, and then Sir Lavaine demanded litters for the wounded Knights, that they might be carried to Westminster with as little hurt as might be. And the Queen and her ladies followed. When they arrived, the Knights told of their adventure, and how Sir Meliagraunce had accused the Queen of treason, and how he and Sir Lancelot were to fight for her good name in eight days.

'Sir Meliagraunce has taken a great deal upon him,' said the King, 'but where is Sir Lancelot?'

'Sir,' answered they all, 'we know not, but we think he has ridden to some adventure.' 'Well, leave him alone,' said the King. 'He will be here when the day comes, unless some treason has befallen him.'

All this while Sir Lancelot was lying in great pain within the cave, and he would have died for lack of food had not one of the ladies in the castle found out the place where he was held captive, and brought him meat and drink, and hoped that he might be brought to love her. But he would not. 'Sir Lancelot,' said she, 'you are not wise, for without my help you will never get out of this prison, and if you do not appear on the day of battle, your lady, Queen Guenevere, will be burnt in default.' 'If I am not there,' replied Sir Lancelot, 'the King and the Queen and all men of worship will know that I am either dead or in prison. And sure I am that there is some good Knight who loves me or is of my kin, that will take my quarrel in hand, therefore you cannot frighten me by such words as these. If there was not another woman in the world, I could give you no different answer.' 'Then you will be shamed openly,' replied the lady, and left the dungeon. But on the day that the battle was to be fought she came again, and said, 'Sir Lancelot, if you will only kiss me once, I will deliver you, and give you the best horse in Sir Meliagraunce's stable.' 'Yes, I will kiss you,' answered Sir Lancelot, 'since I may do that honourably ; but if I thought it were any shame to kiss you, I would not do it, whatever the cost.' So he kissed her, and she brought him his armour, and led him to a stable where twelve noble horses stood, and bade him choose the best. He chose a white courser, and bade the keepers put on the best saddle they had, and with his spear in his hand and his sword by his side, he rode away, thanking the lady for all she had done for him, which some day he would try to repay.

As the hours passed on and Sir Lancelot did not come, Sir Meliagraunce called ever on King Arthur to burn the Queen, or else bring forth Sir Lancelot, for he deemed full well that he had Sir Lancelot safe in his dungeon. The King and Queen were sore distressed that Sir Lancelot was missing, and knew not where to look for him, and what to do. Then stepped forth Sir Lavaine and said, 'My lord Arthur, you know well that some ill-fortune has happened to Sir Lancelot, and if he is not dead, he is either sick or in prison. Therefore I beseech you, let me do battle instead of my lord and master for my lady the Queen.'

'I thank you heartily, gentle Knight,' answered Arthur, 'for I am sure that Sir Meliagraunce accuses the Queen falsely, and there is not one of the ten Knights who would not fight for her were it not for his wounds. So do your best, for it is plain that some evil has been wrought on Sir Lancelot.' Sir Lavaine was filled with joy when the King gave him leave to do battle with Sir Meliagraunce, and rode swiftly to his place at the end of the lists. And just as the heralds were about to cry 'Lesses les aler !' Sir Lancelot dashed into the middle

on his white horse. 'Hold and abide!' commanded the
King, and Sir Lancelot rode up before him, and told
before them all how Sir Meliagraunce had treated him.
When the King and Queen and all the Lords heard Sir
Lancelot's tale, their hearts stirred within them with anger,
and the Queen took her seat by the King, in great trust of
her champion. Sir Lancelot and Sir Meliagraunce prepared themselves for battle, and took their spears, and
came together as thunder, and Sir Lancelot bore Sir Meliagraunce right over his horse. Then Sir Lancelot jumped
down, and they fought on foot, till in the end Sir Meliagraunce was smitten to the ground by a blow on his head
from his enemy. 'Most noble Knight, save my life,' cried
he, 'for I yield myself unto you, and put myself into the
King's hands and yours.' Sir Lancelot did not know
what to answer, for he longed above anything in the
world to have revenge upon him; so he looked at the
Queen to see whether she would give him any sign of
what she would have done. The Queen wagged her head
in answer, and Sir Lancelot knew by that token that she
would have him dead, and he understood, and bade Sir
Meliagraunce get up, and continue the fight. 'Nay,' said
Sir Meliagraunce, 'I will never rise till you accept my
surrender.' 'Listen,' answered Sir Lancelot. 'I will
leave my head and left side bare, and my left arm shall
be bound behind me, and in this guise I will fight with
you.' At this Sir Meliagraunce started to his feet, and
cried, 'My lord Arthur, take heed to this offer, for I will
take it, therefore let him be bound and unarmed as he
has said.' So the Knights disarmed Sir Lancelot, first
his head and then his side, and his left hand was bound
behind his back, in such a manner that he could not use
his shield, and full many a Knight and lady marvelled that
Sir Lancelot would risk himself so. And Sir Meliagraunce
lifted his sword on high and would have smitten Sir
Lancelot on his bare head, had he not leapt lightly to
one side, and, before Sir Meliagraunce could right himself,

Sir Lancelot had struck him so hard upon his helmet that his skull split in two, and there was nothing left to do but to carry his dead body from the field. And because the Knights of the Round Table begged to have him honourably buried, the King agreed thereto, and on his tomb mention was made of how he came by his death, and who slew him. After this Sir Lancelot was more cherished by the King and Queen than ever he was before.

Among the many Knights at Arthur's Court who owned Kings for their fathers were Sir Mordred and Sir Agrawaine, who had for brothers, Sir Gawaine, Sir Gaheris, and Sir Gareth. And their mother was Queen of Orkney, sister to King Arthur. Now Sir Agrawaine and Sir Mordred had evil natures, and loved both to invent slanders and to repeat them. And at this time they were full of envy of the noble deeds Sir Lancelot had done, and how men called him the bravest Knight of the Table Round, and said that he was the friend of the King, and the sworn defender of the Queen. So they cast about how they might ruin him, and found the way by putting jealous thoughts into the mind of Arthur.

As was told in the tale of the marriage of Arthur, Queen Guenevere's heart had gone out to Lancelot, on the journey to the Court, and ever she loved to have him with her. This was known well to Sir Mordred, who watched eagerly for a chance to work her ill.

It came one day when Arthur proclaimed a hunt, and Sir Mordred guessed that Sir Lancelot, who did not love hunting, would stay behind, and would spend the time holding talk with the Queen. Therefore he went to the King and began to speak evil of the Queen and Sir Lancelot. At first King Arthur would listen to nothing, but slowly his jealousy burned within him, and he let the ill words that accused the Queen of loving Sir Lancelot the best, sink into his mind, and told Sir Mordred and Sir Agrawaine that they might do their worst, and he would not meddle

with them. But they let so many of their fellowship into
the secret of their foul plot, that at last it came to the
ears of Sir Bors, who begged Sir Lancelot not to go near
the Queen that day, or harm would come of it. But Sir
Lancelot answered that the Queen had sent for him, and
that she was his liege lady, and never would he hold back
when she summoned him to her presence. Therefore Sir
Bors went heavily away. By ill fortune, Sir Lancelot
only wore his sword under his great mantle, and scarcely
had he passed inside the door when Sir Agrawaine and
Sir Mordred, and twelve other Knights of the Table
Round, all armed and ready for battle, cried loudly upon
Sir Lancelot, that all the Court might hear.

'Madam,' said Sir Lancelot, 'is there any armour
within your chamber that I might cover my body withal,
for if I was armed as they are I would soon crush them ?'

'Alas!' replied the Queen, 'I have neither sword nor
spear nor armour, and how can you resist them? You
will be slain and I shall be burnt. If you could only escape
their hands, I know you would deliver me from danger.'

'It is grievous,' said Sir Lancelot, 'that I who was
never conquered in all my life should be slain for lack of
armour.'

'Traitor Knight,' cried Sir Mordred again, 'come out
and fight us, for you are so sore beset that you cannot
escape us.'

'Oh, mercy,' cried Sir Lancelot, 'I may not suffer
longer this shame and noise ! For better were death at
once than to endure this pain.' Then he took the Queen
in his arms and kissed her, and said, 'Most noble Christian
Queen, I beseech you, as you have ever been my special
good lady, and I at all times your true poor Knight, and
as I never failed you in right or in wrong, since the first
day that King Arthur made me Knight, that you will
pray for my soul, if I be here slain. For I am well
assured that Sir Bors, my nephew, and Sir Lavaine and
many more, will rescue you from the fire, and therefore,

mine own lady, comfort yourself whatever happens to me, and go with Sir Bors, my nephew, and you shall live like a Queen on my lands.'

LANCELOT COMES OVT OF GVENEVERE'S ROOM

'Nay, Lancelot,' said the Queen, 'I will never live after your days, but if you are slain I will take my death as meekly as ever did any Christian Queen.'

'Well, Madam,' answered Lancelot, 'since it is so I shall sell my life as dear as I may, and a thousandfold I am more heavy for you than for myself.'

Therewith Sir Lancelot wrapped his mantle thickly round his arm, and stood beside the door, which the Knights without were trying to break in by aid of a stout wooden form.

'Fair Lords,' said Sir Lancelot, 'leave this noise, and I will open the door, and you may do with me what you will.'

'Open it then,' answered they, 'for well you know you cannot escape us, and we will save your life and bring you before King Arthur.' So Sir Lancelot opened the door and held it with his left hand, so that but one man could come in at once. Then came forward a strong Knight, Sir Colgrevance of Gore, who struck fiercely at Lancelot with his sword. But Sir Lancelot stepped on one side, that the blow fell harmless, and with his arm he gave Sir Colgrevance a buffet on the head so that he fell dead. And Sir Lancelot drew him into the chamber, and barred the door.

Hastily he unbuckled the dead Knight's armour, and the Queen and her ladies put it on him, Sir Agrawaine and Sir Mordred ever calling to him the while, 'Traitor Knight, come out of that chamber!' But Sir Lancelot cried to them all to go away and he would appear next morning before the King, and they should accuse him of what they would, and he would answer them, and prove his words in battle. 'Fie on you, traitor,' said Sir Agrawaine, 'we have you in our power, to save or to slay, for King Arthur will listen to our words, and will believe what we tell him.'

'As you like,' answered Sir Lancelot, 'look to yourself,' and he flung open the chamber door, and strode in amongst them and killed Sir Agrawaine with his first blow, and in a few minutes the bodies of the other twelve Knights lay on the ground beside his, for no man ever withstood that buffet of Sir Lancelot's. He wounded Sir Mordred also, so that he fled away with all his might. When the clamour of the battle was still, Sir Lancelot turned back to the Queen and said, 'Alas, Madam, they will make King Arthur my foe, and yours also, but if you will come with me to my castle, I will save you from all dangers.'

'I will not go with you now,' answered the Queen, 'but if you see to-morrow that they will burn me to death, then you may deliver me as you shall think best.'

'While I live I will deliver you,' said Sir Lancelot, and he left her and went back to his lodging. When Sir Bors, who was awaiting him, saw Sir Lancelot, he was gladder than he ever had been in his whole life before. 'Mercy!' cried Sir Lancelot, 'why you are all armed!'

'Sir,' answered Sir Bors, 'after you had left us I and your friends and your kinsmen were so troubled that we felt some great strife was at hand, and that perchance some trap had been laid for you. So we put on armour that we might help you whatever need you were in.'

'Fair nephew,' said Lancelot, 'but now I have been more hardly beset than ever I was in my life, and yet I escaped,' and he told them all that had happened. 'I pray you, my fellows, that you will be of good courage and stand by me in my need, for war is come to us all.'

'Sir,' answered Sir Bors, 'all is welcome that God sends us, and we have had much good with you and much fame, so now we will take the bad as we have taken the good.' And so said they all.

'I thank you for your comfort in my great distress,' replied Sir Lancelot, 'and you, fair nephew, haste to the Knights which be in this place, and find who is with me and who is against me, for I would know my friends from my foes.'

'Sir,' said Sir Bors, 'before seven of the clock in the morning you shall know.'

By seven o'clock, as Sir Bors had promised, many

noble Knights stood before Sir Lancelot, and were sworn
to his cause. ' My Lords,' said he, 'you know well that
since I came into this country I have given faithful
service unto my lord King Arthur and unto my lady
Queen Guenevere. Last evening my lady, the Queen,
sent for me to speak to her, and certain Knights that
were lying in wait for me cried " Treason," and much ado
I had to escape their blows. But I slew twelve of them,
and Sir Agrawaine, who is Sir Gawaine's brother; and
for this cause I am sure of mortal war, as these Knights
were ordered by King Arthur to betray me, and therefore the Queen will be judged to the fire, and I may not
suffer that she should be burnt for my sake.'

And Sir Bors answered Sir Lancelot that it was truly
his part to rescue the Queen, as he had done so often
before, and that if she was burned the shame would be
his. Then they all took counsel together how the thing
might best be done, and Sir Bors deemed it wise to carry
her off to the Castle of Joyous Gard, and counselled that
she should be kept there, a prisoner, till the King's
anger was past and he would be willing to welcome
her back again. To this the other Knights agreed, and
by the advice of Sir Lancelot they hid themselves in a
wood close by the town till they saw what King Arthur
would do. Meanwhile Sir Mordred, who had managed
to escape the sword of Sir Lancelot, rode, wounded and
bleeding, unto King Arthur, and told the King all that
had passed, and how, of the fourteen Knights, he only
was left alive. The King grieved sore at his tale, which
Sir Mordred had made to sound as ill as was possible;
for, in spite of all, Arthur loved Sir Lancelot. ' It is a
bitter blow,' he said, 'that Sir Lancelot must be against
me, and the fellowship of the Table Round is broken for
ever, as many a noble Knight will go with him. And as
I am the judge, the Queen will have to die, as she is the
cause of the death of these thirteen Knights.'

'My lord Arthur,' said Sir Gawaine, ' be not over-hasty; listen not to the foul tongue of Sir Mordred, who laid this trap for Sir Lancelot, that we all know to be the Queen's own Knight, who has done battle for her when none else would. As for Sir Lancelot, he will prove the right on the body of any Knight living that shall accuse him of wrong — either him, or my lady Guenevere.'

'That I believe well,' said King Arthur, 'for he trusts so much in his own might that he fears no man; and never more shall he fight for the Queen, for she must suffer death by the law. Put on, therefore, your best armour, and go with your brothers, Sir Gaheris and Sir Gareth, and bring the Queen to the fire, there to have her judgment and suffer her death.'

'Nay, my lord, that I will never do,' cried Sir Gawaine; 'my heart will never serve me to see her die, and I will never stand by and see so noble a lady brought to a shameful end.'

'Then,' said the King, 'let your brothers, Sir Gaheris and Sir Gareth, be there.'

'My lord,' replied Sir Gawaine, 'I know well how loth they will be, but they are young and unable to say you nay.'

At this Sir Gaheris and Sir Gareth spoke to King Arthur: 'Sir, if you command us we will obey, but it will be sore against our will. And if we go we shall be dressed as men of peace, and wear no armour.'

'Make yourselves ready, then,' answered the King, 'for I would delay no longer in giving judgment.'

'Alas!' cried Sir Gawaine, 'that I should have lived to see this day'; and he turned and wept bitterly, and went into his chamber.

So the Queen was led outside the gates, and her rich dress was taken off, while her lords and ladies wrung their hands in grief, and few men wore armour, for in that day it was held that the presence of mail-clad Knights made death more shameful. Now among those present was one sent by Sir Lancelot, and when he saw the Queen's dress unclasped, and the priest step forth to listen to her confession, he rode to warn Sir Lancelot that the hour had come. And suddenly there was heard a sound as of rushing horses, and Sir Lancelot dashed up to the fire, and all the Knights that stood around were slain, for few men wore armour. Sir Lancelot looked not where he struck, and Sir Gaheris and Sir Gareth were found in the thickest of the throng. At last he reached the Queen, and, throwing a mantle over her, he caught her on to his saddle and rode away with her. Right thankful was the Queen at being snatched from the fire, and her heart was grateful to Sir Lancelot, who took her to his Castle of Joyous Gard, and many noble Knights and Kings had fellowship with them.

After King Arthur had given judgment for the Queen to die he went back into his palace of Westminster, where men came and told him how Sir Lancelot had delivered her, and of the death of his Knights, and in especial of Sir Gaheris and Sir Gareth, and he swooned away from sorrow. 'Alas!' he cried, when he recovered from his swoon, 'alas! that a crown was ever on my head, for in these two days I have lost forty Knights and the fellowship of Sir Lancelot and his kinsmen, and never more will they be of my company. But I charge you that none tell Sir Gawaine of the death of his brothers, for I am sure that when he hears of Sir Gareth he will go out of his mind. Oh, why did Sir Lancelot slay them? for Sir Gareth loved Sir Lancelot more than any other man.'

'That is true,' answered some of the Knights, 'but Sir Lancelot saw not whom he smote, and therefore were they slain.'

'The death of those two,' said Arthur, 'will cause the greatest mortal war that ever was. I am sure that when Sir Gawaine knows Sir Gareth is slain he will never suffer me to rest till I have destroyed Sir Lancelot and all his kin, or till they have destroyed me. My heart was never so heavy as it is now, and far more grievous to me is the loss of my good Knights than of my Queen; for Queens I might have in plenty, but no man had ever such a company of Knights, and it hurts me sore that Sir Lancelot and I should be at war. It is the ill will borne by Sir Agrawaine and Sir Mordred to Sir Lancelot that has caused all this sorrow.' Then one came to Sir Gawaine and told him that Sir Lancelot had borne off the Queen, and that twenty-four Knights had been slain in the combat. 'I knew well he would deliver her,' said Sir Gawaine, 'and in that, he has but acted as a Knight should and as I would have done myself. But where are my brethren? I marvel they have not been to seek me.'

'Truly,' said the man, 'Sir Gaheris and Sir Gareth are slain.'

'Heaven forbid any such thing,' returned Sir Gawaine. 'I would not for all the world that that had happened, especially to my brother, Sir Gareth.'

'He is slain,' said the man, 'and it is grievous news.'

'Who slew him?' asked Sir Gawaine.

'Sir Lancelot slew them both,' answered the man.

'He cannot have slain Sir Gareth,' replied Sir Gawaine, 'for my brother Gareth loved him better than me and all his brethren, and King Arthur too. And had Sir Lancelot desired my brother to go with him, he would have turned his back on us all. Therefore I can never believe that Sir Lancelot slew my brother.'

'Sir, it is in everyone's mouth,' said the man. At this Sir Gawaine fell back in a swoon and lay long as if he were dead. Then he ran to the King, crying, 'O King Arthur, mine uncle, my good brother Sir Gareth is slain, and Sir Gaheris also,' and the King wept with him. At length Sir Gawaine said, 'Sir, I will go and see my brother Sir Gareth.'

'You cannot do that,' returned the King, 'for I have

caused him to be buried with Sir Gaheris, as I knew well
that the sight would cause you overmuch sorrow.'

'How came he, Sir Lancelot, to slay Sir Gareth?'
asked Sir Gawaine; 'mine own good lord, I pray you
tell me, for neither Sir Gareth nor Sir Gaheris bore arms
against him.'

'It is said,' answered the King, 'that Sir Lancelot
slew them in the thickest of the press and knew them
not. Therefore let us think upon a plan to avenge their
deaths.'

'My King, my lord and mine uncle,' said Sir Gawaine,
'I swear to you by my knighthood that from this day I
will never rest until Sir Lancelot or I be slain. And I
will go to the world's end till I find him.'

'You need not seek him so far,' answered the King,
'for I am told that Sir Lancelot will await me and you
in the Castle of Joyous Gard, and many people are flocking to him. But call your friends together, and I will
call mine,' and the King ordered letters to be sent
throughout all England summoning his Knights and vas-
sals to the siege of Joyous Gard. The Castle of Joyous
Gard was strong, and after fifteen weeks had passed no
breach had been made in its walls. And one day, at the
time of harvest, Sir Lancelot came forth on a truce, and
the King and Sir Gawaine challenged him to do battle.

'Nay,' answered Sir Lancelot, 'with yourself I will
never strive, and I grieve sorely that I have slain your
Knights. But I was forced to it, for the saving of my
life and that of my lady the Queen. And except yourself, my lord, and Sir Gawaine, there is no man that
shall call me traitor but he shall pay for it with his body.
As to Queen Guenevere, oft times, my lord, you have
consented in the heat of your passion that she should be
burnt and destroyed, and it fell to me to do battle for
her, and her enemies confessed their untruth, and acknowledged her innocent. And at such times, my lord
Arthur, you loved me and thanked me when I saved your

Queen from the fire, and promised ever to be my good lord, for I have fought for her many times in other quarrels than my own. Therefore, my gracious lord, take your Queen back into your grace again.'

To these words of Sir Lancelot's King Arthur answered nothing, but in his heart he would fain have made peace with Sir Lancelot, but Sir Gawaine would not let him. He reproached Sir Lancelot bitterly for the deaths of his brothers and kinsmen, and called Sir Lancelot a craven and other ill names that he would not fight with King Arthur. So at the last Sir Lancelot's patience and courtesy failed him, and he told them that the next morning he would give them battle.

The heart of Sir Gawaine leaped with joy when he heard these words of Sir Lancelot, and he summoned all his friends and his kinsfolk, and bade them watch well Sir Lancelot, and to slay him if a chance offered. But he knew not that Sir Lancelot had bidden the Knights of his following in no wise to touch King Arthur or Sir Gawaine. And when the dawn broke a great host marched out of the Castle of Joyous Gard, with Sir Lancelot at the head, and Sir Bors and Sir Lionel commanding on either side. All that day they fought, and sometimes one army seemed to be gaining, and sometimes the other. Many times King Arthur drew near Sir Lancelot, and would have slain him, and Sir Lancelot suffered him, and would not strike again. But the King was unhorsed by Sir Bors, and would have been slain but for Sir Lancelot, who stayed his hand. 'My lord Arthur,' he said, 'for God's love stop this strife. I cannot strike you, so you will gain no fame by it, though your friends never cease from trying to slay me. My lord, remember what I have done in many places and how evil is now my reward.' Then when King Arthur was on his horse again he looked on Sir Lancelot, and tears burst from his eyes, thinking of the great courtesy that was in Sir Lancelot more than in any other man. He sighed to himself, saying softly, 'Alas ! that ever this war began,' and rode away, while the battle ended for that time and the dead were buried.

But Sir Gawaine would not suffer the King to make peace, and they fought on, now in one place, and now in another, till the Pope heard of the strife and sent a noble clerk, the Bishop of Rochester, to charge the King to make peace with Sir Lancelot, and to take back unto him his Queen, the Lady Guenevere. Now the King, as has been said, would fain have followed the Pope's counsel and have accorded with Sir Lancelot, but Sir Gawaine would not suffer him. However, as to the Queen Sir Gawaine said nothing; and King Arthur gave audience to the Bishop, and swore on his great seal that he would take back the Queen as the Pope desired, and that if Sir Lancelot brought her he should come safe and go safe. So the Bishop rode to Joyous Gard and showed Sir Lancelot what the Pope had written and King Arthur had answered, and told him of the perils which would befall him if he withheld the Queen. 'It was never in my thought,' answered Sir Lancelot, 'to withhold the Queen from King Arthur, but as she would have been dead for my sake it was my part to save her life, and to keep her from danger till better times came. And I thank God that the Pope has made peace, and I shall be a thousand times gladder to bring her back than I was to take her away. Therefore ride to the King, and say that in eight days I myself will bring the Lady Guenevere unto him.' So the Bishop departed, and came to the King at Carlisle and told him what Sir Lancelot had answered, and tears burst from the King's eyes once more.

A goodly host of a hundred Knights rode eight days later from the Castle of Joyous Gard; every Knight was clothed in green velvet, and held in his hand a branch of olive, and bestrode a horse with trappings down to his heels. And behind the Queen were four and twenty gentlewomen clad in green likewise, while twelve esquires

attended on Sir Lancelot. He and the Queen wore dresses
of white and gold tissue, and their horses were clothed
in housings of the same, set with precious stones and
pearls ; and no man had ever gazed on such a noble pair,
as they rode from Joyous Gard to Carlisle. When they
reached the castle, Sir Lancelot sprang from his horse
and helped the Queen from hers, and led her to where
King Arthur sat, with Sir Gawaine and many Lords
around him. He kneeled down, and the Queen kneeled
with him, and many Knights wept as though it had been
their own kin. But Arthur sat still and said nothing.
At that Sir Lancelot rose, and the Queen likewise, and,
looking straight at the King, he spoke :

'Most noble King, I have brought to you my lady the
Queen, as right requires ; and time hath been, my lord
Arthur, that you have been greatly pleased with me when
I did battle for my lady your Queen. And full well you
know that she has been put to great wrong ere this, and
it seems to me I had more cause to deliver her from this
fire, seeing she would have been burnt for my sake.'

'Well, well, Sir Lancelot,' said the King, 'I have given
you no cause to do to me as you have done, for I have
held you dearer than any of my Knights.' But Sir
Gawaine would not suffer the King to listen to anything
Sir Lancelot said, and told him roughly that while one
of them lived peace could never be made, and desired on
behalf of the King that in fifteen days he should be gone
out of the country. And still King Arthur said nothing,
but suffered Sir Gawaine to talk as he would ; and Sir
Lancelot took farewell of him and of the Queen, and
rode, grieving sorely, out of the Court, and sailed to his
lands beyond the sea.

Though the Queen was returned again, and Sir Lancelot was beyond the sea, the hate of Sir Gawaine towards
him was in no way set at rest, but he raised a great host
and persuaded the King to follow him. And after many

sieges and long fighting Sir Gawaine did battle with Sir Lancelot once more, and was worsted, and Sir Lancelot might have slain him, but would not. While he lay wounded tidings came to King Arthur from England that caused the King to give up his war with Sir Lancelot and return in all haste to his own country.

THE END OF IT ALL

Now when King Arthur left England to fight with Sir Lancelot he ordered his nephew Sir Mordred to govern the land, which that false Knight did gladly. And as soon as he thought he might safely do so he caused some letters to be written saying that King Arthur had been slain in battle, and he had himself crowned King at Canterbury, where he made a great feast which lasted fifteen days. After it was over, he went to Winchester and summoned Queen Guenevere, and told her that on a certain day he would wed her and that she should make herself ready. Queen Guenevere's soul grew cold and heavy as she heard these words of Sir Mordred's, for she hated him with all her might, as he hated her; but she dared show nothing, and answered softly that she would do his bidding, only she desired that first she might go to London to buy all manner of things for her wedding. Sir Mordred trusted her because of her fair speech, and let her go. Then the Queen rode to London with all speed, and went straight to the Tower, which she filled in haste with food, and called her men-at-arms round her. When Sir Mordred knew how she had beguiled him he was wroth out of measure, and besieged the Tower, and assaulted it many times with battering rams and great engines, but could prevail nothing, for the Queen would never, for fair speech nor for foul, give herself into his hands again.

The Bishop of Canterbury hastened unto Sir Mordred, and rebuked him for wishing to marry his uncle's wife.

'Leave such desires,' said the Bishop, 'or else I shall curse you with bell, book, and candle. Also, you noise abroad that my lord Arthur is slain, and that is not so, and therefore you will make ill work in the land.' At this Sir Mordred waxed very wroth, and would have killed the Bishop had he not fled to Glastonbury, where he became a hermit, and lived in poverty and prayed all day long for the realm, for he knew that a fierce war was at hand. Soon word came to Sir Mordred that King Arthur was hurrying home across the seas, to be avenged on his nephew, who had proved traitor. Wherefore Sir Mordred sent letters to all the people throughout the kingdom, and many followed after him, for he had cunningly sown among them that with him was great joy and softness of life, while King Arthur would bring war and strife with him. So Sir Mordred drew with a great host to Dover, and waited for the King. Before King Arthur and his men could land from the boats and ships that had brought them over the sea Sir Mordred set upon them, and there was heavy slaughter. But in the end he and his men were driven back, and he fled, and his people with him. After the fight was over the King ordered the dead to be buried; and there came a man and told him that he had found Sir Gawaine lying in a boat, and that he was sore wounded. And the King went to him, and made moan over him : 'You were ever the man in the world that I loved most,' said he ; 'you and Sir Lancelot.' 'Mine uncle King Arthur,' answered Sir Gawaine, 'my death day has come, and all through my own fault. Had Sir Lancelot been with you as he used to be this unhappy war had never begun, and of that I am the cause, for I would not accord with him. And therefore, I pray you, give me paper, pen, and ink that I may write to him.' So paper and ink were brought, and Sir Gawaine was held up by King Arthur, and a letter was writ wherein Sir Gawaine confessed that he was dying of an old wound given him

by Sir Lancelot in the siege of one of the cities across
the sea, and thus was fulfilled the prophecy of Merlin.
'Of a more noble man might I not be slain,' said he.
'Also, Sir Lancelot, make no tarrying, but come in haste
to King Arthur, for sore bested is he with my brother
Sir Mordred, who has taken the crown, and would have
wedded my lady Queen Guenevere had she not sought
safety in the Tower of London. Pray for my soul, I
beseech you, and visit my tomb.' And after writing this
letter, at the hour of noon, Sir Gawaine gave up his
spirit, and was buried by the King in the chapel within
Dover Castle. Then was it told King Arthur that Sir
Mordred had pitched a new field upon Barham Down,
and the next morning the King rode hither to him, and
there was a fierce battle between them, and many on
both sides were slain. But at the last King Arthur's
party stood best, and Sir Mordred and his men fled to
Canterbury.

After the Knights which were dead had been buried,
and those that were wounded tended with healing salves,
King Arthur drew westwards towards Salisbury, and
many of Sir Mordred's men followed after him, but they
that loved Sir Lancelot went unto Sir Mordred. And a
day was fixed between the King and Sir Mordred that
they should meet upon a down near Salisbury, and give
battle once more. But the night before the battle Sir
Gawaine appeared unto the King in a vision, and warned
him not to fight next day, which was Trinity Sunday, as
he would be slain and many of his Knights also; but to
make a truce for a month, and at the end of that time Sir
Lancelot would arrive, and would slay Sir Mordred, and
all his Knights with him. As soon as he awoke the
King called the Bishops and the wisest men of his army,
and told them of his vision, and took counsel what
should be done. And it was agreed that the King should
send an embassage of two Knights and two Bishops unto
Sir Mordred, and offer him as much goods and lands as

they thought best if he would engage to make a treaty for a month with King Arthur.

So they departed, and came to Sir Mordred, where he had a grim host of an hundred thousand men. For a long time he would not suffer himself to be entreated, but at the last he agreed to have Cornwall and Kent in King Arthur's days, and after all England. Furthermore, it was decided that King Arthur and Sir Mordred should meet in the plain between their hosts, each with fourteen persons. 'I am glad of this,' said King Arthur, when he heard what had been done; but he warned his men that if they were to see a sword drawn they were to come on swiftly and slay that traitor, Sir Mordred, 'for I in no wise trust him.' And in like wise spake Sir Mordred unto his host. Then they two met, and agreed on the truce, and wine was fetched and they drank, and all was well. But while they were drinking an adder crept out of a bush, and stung one of the fourteen Knights on his foot, and he drew his sword to slay the adder, not thinking of anything but his pain. And when the men of both armies beheld that drawn sword, they blew trumpets and horns and shouted grimly, and made them ready for battle. So King Arthur leaped on his horse, and Sir Mordred on his, and they went back to their own armies, and thus began the fight, and never was there seen one more doleful in any Christian land. For all day long there was rushing and riding, spearing and striking, and many a grim word was there spoken, and many a deadly stroke given. And at the end full an hundred thousand dead men lay upon the down, and King Arthur had but two Knights left living, Sir Lucan and his brother, Sir Bedivere. 'Alas! that I should have lived to see this day,' cried the King, 'for now I am come to mine end; but would to God that I knew where were that traitor Sir Mordred that hath caused all this mischief.' Then suddenly he saw Sir Mordred leaning on his sword among a great heap of dead men.

'Give me my spear,' said King Arthur unto Sir Lucan.

'Sir, let him be,' answered Sir Lucan. 'Remember your dream, and leave off by this. For, blessed be God, you have won the field, and we three be alive, and of the others none is alive save Sir Mordred himself. If you leave off now, the day of destiny is past.'

'Tide me death, tide me life,' said the King, 'he shall not escape my hands, for a better chance I shall never have,' and he took his spear in both hands and ran towards Sir Mordred, crying 'Traitor! now is your death day come,' and smote him under the shield, so that the spear went through his body. And when Sir Mordred felt he had his death wound, he raised himself up and struck King Arthur such a blow that the sword clave his helmet, and then fell stark dead on the earth again. When Sir Lucan and Sir Bedivere saw that sight they carried the King to a little chapel, but they hoped not to leave him there long, for Sir Lucan had noted that many people were stealing out to rob the slain of the ornaments on their armour. And those that were not dead already they slew.

'Would that I could quit this place to go to some large town,' said the King, when he had heard this, 'but I cannot stand, my head works so. Ah, Lancelot, sorely have I missed thee.' At that Sir Lucan and Sir Bedivere tried to lift him, but Sir Lucan had been grievously wounded in the fight, and the blood burst forth again as he lifted Arthur, and he died and fell at the feet of the King.

'Alas!' said the King, 'he has died for my sake, and he had more need of help than I. But he would not complain, his heart was so set to help me. And I should sorrow yet more if I were still to live long, but my time flieth fast. Therefore, Sir Bedivere, cease moaning and weeping, and take Excalibur, my good sword, and go with it to yonder water side, and when thou comest there, I charge thee, throw my sword in that water, and come again and tell me what thou hast seen.'

THE LAST
BATTLE

H J FORD

Sir Mordred

'My lord,' answered Sir Bedivere, 'your commandment shall be done,' and he departed. But when he looked at that noble sword, and beheld the jewels and gold that covered the pommel and hilt, he said to himself, 'If I throw this rich sword into the water no good will come of it, but only harm and loss'; so he hid Excalibur under a tree, and returned unto the King and told him his bidding was done. 'What did you see there?' asked the King.

'Sir,' answered Sir Bedivere, 'I saw nothing but the winds and waves.'

'You have not dealt truly with me,' said the King. 'Go back, and do my command; spare not, but throw it in.' But again Sir Bedivere's heart failed him, and he hid the sword, and returned to tell the King he had seen nothing but the wan water.

'Ah, traitor!' cried King Arthur, 'this is twice you have betrayed me. If you do not now fulfil my bidding, with mine own hands will I slay you, for you would gladly see me dead for the sake of my sword.' Then Sir Bedivere was shamed at having disobeyed the King, and drew forth the sword from its hiding place, and carried it to the water side, and with a mighty swing threw it far into the water. And as it flew through the air, an arm and hand lifted itself out of the water, and caught the hilt, and brandished the sword thrice, and vanished with it beneath the water. So Sir Bedivere came again unto the King, and told him what he saw.

'Alas!' said the King, 'help me hence, for I have tarried overlong,' and Sir Bedivere took him on his back, and bare him to the water side. And when they stood by the bank, a little barge containing many fair ladies and a Queen, all in black hoods, drew near, and they wept and shrieked when they beheld King Arthur.

'Now put me into the barge,' said the King, and Sir Bedivere laid him softly down, and the ladies made great mourning and the barge rowed from the land.

'Ah, my lord Arthur!' cried Sir Bedivere, 'what shall become of me now you go from me, and I am left here alone with my enemies?'

'Comfort yourself,' replied the King, 'and do as well as you may, for I go unto the valley of Avilion, to be healed of my grievous wound. And if you never more hear of me, pray for my soul.' But Sir Bedivere watched the barge till it was beyond his sight, then he rode all night till he came to a hermitage. Now when Queen Guenevere heard of the battle, and how that King Arthur was slain and Sir Mordred and all their Knights, she stole away, and five ladies with her, and rode to Amesbury; and there she put on clothes of black and white, and became a nun, and did great penance, and many alms deeds, and people marvelled at her and at her godly life. And ever she wept and moaned over the years that were past, and for King Arthur.

As soon as the messenger whom the King had sent with Sir Gawaine's letter reached Sir Lancelot, and he learned that Sir Mordred had taken for himself the crown of England, he rose up in wrath, and, calling Sir Bors, bid him collect their host, that they should pass at once over the sea to avenge themselves on that false Knight. A fair wind blew them to Dover, and there Sir Lancelot asked tidings of King Arthur. Then the people told him that the King was slain, and Sir Mordred, and an hundred thousand men besides, and that the King had buried Sir Gawaine in the chapel at Dover Castle. 'Fair Sirs,' said Sir Lancelot, 'show me that tomb'; and they showed it to him, and Sir Lancelot kneeled before it, and wept and prayed, and this he did for two days. And on the third morning he summoned before him all the great Lords and leaders of his host, and said to them, 'Fair Lords, I thank you all for coming here with me, but we come too late, and that will be bitter grief to me as long as I shall live. But since it is so, I will myself ride and seek my lady Guenevere in the west country, where they say she has

EXCALIBVR RETVRNS TO THE MERE

gone, and tarry you here, I entreat you, for fifteen days, and if I should not return take your ships and depart into your own country.'

Sir Bors strove to reason with him that the quest was fruitless, and that in the west country he would find few friends; but his words availed nothing. For seven days Sir Lancelot rode, and at last he came to a nunnery, where Queen Guenevere was looking out from her lattice, and was ware of his presence as he walked in the cloister. And when she saw him she swooned, and her ladies and gentlewomen tended her. When she was recovered, she spoke to them and said, ' You will marvel, fair ladies, why I should swoon. It was caused by the sight of yonder Knight who stands there, and I pray you bring him to me.' As soon as Sir Lancelot was brought she said to her ladies, 'Through me and this man has this war been wrought, for which I repent me night and day. Therefore, Sir Lancelot, I require and pray you never to see my face again, but go back to your own land, and govern it and protect it; and take to yourself a wife, and pray that my soul may be made clean of its ill doing.'

'Nay, Madam,' answered Sir Lancelot, 'that shall I never do; but the same life that you have taken upon you, will I take upon me likewise.'

'If you will do so,' said the Queen, 'it is well; but I may never believe but that you will turn to the world again.'

'Well, Madam,' answered he, 'you speak as it pleases you, but you never knew me false to my promise, and I will forsake the world as you have done. For if in the quest of the Sangreal I had forsaken its vanities with all my heart and will, I had passed all Knights in the quest, except Sir Galahad my son. And therefore, lady, since you have taken you to perfection, I must do so also, and if I may find a hermit that will receive me I will pray and do penance while my life lasts. Wherefore, Madam, I beseech you to kiss me once again.'

'No,' said the Queen, 'that I may not do,' and Sir Lancelot took his horse and departed in great sorrow. All that day and the next night he rode through the forest till he beheld a hermitage and a chapel between two cliffs, and heard a little bell ring to Mass. And he that sang Mass was the Bishop of Canterbury, and Sir Bedivere was with him. After Mass Sir Bedivere told Sir Lancelot how King Arthur had thrown away his sword and had sailed to the valley of Avilion, and Sir Lancelot's heart almost burst for grief. Then he kneeled down and besought the Bishop that he might be his brother. 'That I will, gladly,' said the Bishop, and put a robe upon him.

After the fifteen days were ended, and still Sir Lancelot did not return, Sir Bors made the great host go back across the sea, while he and some of Sir Lancelot's kin set forth to seek all over England till they found Sir Lancelot. They rode different ways, and by fortune Sir Bors came one day to the chapel where Sir Lancelot was. And he prayed that he might stay and be one of their fellowship, and in six months six other Knights were joined to them, and their horses went where they would, for the Knights spent their lives in fasting and prayer, and kept no riches for themselves.

In this wise six years passed, and one night a vision came to Sir Lancelot in his sleep charging him to hasten unto Amesbury. 'By the time that thou come there,' said the vision, 'thou shalt find Queen Guenevere dead; therefore take thy fellows with thee and fetch her corpse, and bury it by the side of her husband, the noble King Arthur.'

Then Sir Lancelot rose up and told the hermit, and the hermit ordered him to make ready and to do all as the vision had commanded. And Sir Lancelot and seven of the other Knights went on foot from Glastonbury to

Amesbury, and it took them two days to compass the
distance, for it was far and they were weak with fasting.
When they reached the nunnery Queen Guenevere had
been dead but half an hour, and she had first summoned
her ladies to her, and told them that Sir Lancelot had
been a priest for near a twelvemonth. 'And hither he
cometh as fast as he may,' she said, 'to fetch my corpse,
and beside my lord King Arthur he shall bury me. And
I beseech Almighty God that I may never have power to
see Sir Lancelot with my bodily eyes.' 'Thus,' said the
ladies, 'she prayed for two days till she was dead.' Then
Sir Lancelot looked upon her face and sighed, but wept
little, and next day he sang Mass. After that the Queen
was laid on a bier drawn by horses, and an hundred
torches were carried round her, and Sir Lancelot and his
fellows walked behind her singing holy chants, and at
times one would come forward and throw incense on the
dead. So they came to Glastonbury, and the Bishop of
Canterbury sang a Requiem Mass over the Queen, and
she was wrapped in cloth, and placed first in a web of
lead, and then in a coffin of marble, and when she was
put into the earth Sir Lancelot swooned away.

'You are to blame,' said the hermit, when he awaked
from his swoon, 'you ought not make such manner of
sorrow.'

'Truly,' answered Sir Lancelot, 'I trust I do not
displease God, but when I remember her beauty, and
her nobleness, and that of the King, and when I saw his
corpse and her corpse lie together, my heart would not
bear up my body. And I remembered, too, that it was
through me and my pride that they both came to their
end.'

From that day Sir Lancelot ate so little food that he
dwined away, and for the most part was found kneeling
by the tomb of King Arthur and Queen Guenevere.
None could comfort him, and after six weeks he was too
weak to rise from his bed. Then he sent for the hermit

and to his fellows, and asked in a weary voice that they
would give him the last rites of the Church; and begged
that when he was dead his body might be taken to
Joyous Gard, which some say is Alnwick and others
Bamborough.   That night the hermit had a vision that he
saw Sir Lancelot being carried up to heaven by the angels,
and he waked Sir Bors and bade him go and see if
anything ailed Sir Lancelot.   So Sir Bors went and Sir
Lancelot lay on his bed, stark dead, and he smiled as he
lay there.   Then was there great weeping and wringing
of hands, more than had been made for any man; but
they placed him on the horse bier that had carried Queen
Guenevere, and lit a hundred torches, and in fifteen days
they reached Joyous Gard.   There his body was laid in
the choir, with his face uncovered, and many prayers
were said over him.   And there, in the midst of their
praying, came Sir Ector de Maris, who for seven years
had sought Sir Lancelot through all the land.

  'Ah, Lancelot,' he said, when he stood looking beside
his dead body, 'thou wert head of all Christian Knights.
Thou wert the courtliest Knight that ever drew sword,
and the faithfulest friend that ever bestrode a horse.
Thou wert the goodliest Knight that ever man has seen,
and the truest lover that ever loved a woman.'